P9-DEQ-306

Withdrawn

OCT 0 1 2015

Northville District Library
212 W. Cady Street
Northville, MI 48167-1560

WOMAN OF THE DEAD

A NOVEL

BERNHARD AICHNER

SCRIBNER

New York London Toronto Sydney New Delhi

SCRIBNER
An Imprint of Simon & Schuster, Inc.
1230 Avenue of the Americas
New York, NY 10020

This book is a work of fiction. Any references to historical events, real people, or real places are used fictitiously. Other names, characters, places, and events are products of the author's imagination, and any resemblance to actual events or places or persons, living or dead, is entirely coincidental.

Copyright © 2015 by Bernhard Aichner
Translation copyright © 2015 by Anthea Bell

All rights reserved, including the right to reproduce this book or portions thereof in any form whatsoever. For information, address Scribner Subsidiary Rights Department, 1230 Avenue of the Americas, New York, NY 10020.

First Scribner hardcover edition August 2015

SCRIBNER and design are registered trademarks of The Gale Group, Inc., used under license by Simon & Schuster, Inc., the publisher of this work.

For information about special discounts for bulk purchases, please contact Simon & Schuster Special Sales at 1-866-506-1949 or business@simonandschuster.com.

The Simon & Schuster Speakers Bureau can bring authors to your live event. For more information or to book an event, contact the Simon & Schuster Speakers Bureau at 1-866-248-3049 or visit our website at www.simonspeakers.com.

Manufactured in the United States of America

1   3   5   7   9   10   8   6   4   2

Library of Congress Cataloging-in-Publication Data is available.

ISBN 978-1-4767-7561-6
ISBN 978-1-4767-7563-0 (ebook)

If you look down into an abyss for a long time, the abyss looks back at you.

Friedrich Nietzsche

Eight years earlier

You can see it all from above. The sea, the sailing boat, her skin. A naked woman is on deck, the sun is shining and all is well. She simply lies there, looking up, her eyes are open, there's just her and the sky, the clouds. This is the best place in the world: the boat that her parents bought twenty years ago, a marvel, a pearl beyond price, at home in Trieste harbor. Life on the water under the open sky where there's no one else in sight. Only water far and wide, music in her ears, sweat gathering in her navel. Nothing else.

They have been sailing from Trieste to the Kornati Islands, they're in no hurry, there is nothing to do. She has gone on holiday with her parents for so many years now. They'll soon be seventy, tanned by wind and weather, passionately enthusiastic sailors both. They've always gone on sailing holidays, ever since she was small. As a child she wore bathing trunks, then a bikini, she was never naked before.

She undressed two hours ago, and lay down without bothering to apply sunscreen. She wants the sun to burn her, she wants her skin to scream out loud when she is found. She wants to be naked at last. Now, there is no one to tell her off. No father. No mother. She is alone on the boat with her breasts, her hips, her legs, her arms. There's a smile on her lips as she nods in time to the music. At this moment, there's nowhere on earth she would rather be.

She'll lie there for another three hours, stretching out in the sun, soaking up the summer. Another three hours, or four. Until they finally sink. Until they stop calling out. Until they stop flailing at the water, splashing it into the air. Until they fall silent, forever.

It is midday off the Croatian island of Dugi Otok. She doesn't move. She's going to say that she fell asleep, she didn't hear a thing, the music was too loud, the sun made her drowsy. She will answer all the questions she is asked, she will give a full explanation, and she will shed tears. When the time comes, she'll do everything it takes. But for now there is only the sky above her and she traces circles on it, writing in the blue space. She paints her future in the sky, imagining her new life. Now the Institute is hers. She will change everything, modernize it, make it a successful business again. She'll be in charge of everything. She will take the boat back to Trieste and begin all over again.

There's sweat everywhere. How she enjoys being naked. *You are not going to undress, Brünhilde. Not on our boat. Our rules hold good as long as we live, Brünhilde.* But there are no rules now, nothing is forbidden. She has undressed, she is lying on deck stretching out her body. Everything that makes her what she is waves in the wind like a banner, she blossoms in the sun, she is happy. Happier with every minute she spends alone.

Brünhilde Blum is twenty-four years old, the daughter of Hagen and Herta Blum. Adopted daughter. They took her from the children's home when she was three, they trained her like a domestic pet, she was brought up to succeed them. She was Hagen's last hope for the family firm. Even if they could only adopt a girl. A girl or nothing, they were told. The waiting lists were long, and Hagen was desperate. So desperate that he began to contemplate leaving his business in the hands of a woman. She was to carry on the firm that was sacred to him, she was to preserve what he had created, she was to be a substitute man for Hagen's sake. She did everything he demanded, everything required by the profession. The firm of Blum, Funeral Directors, meant the world to him—it mattered more than anything.

It was a traditional business: her prison, her nursery. Founded shortly after the war in 1949, at a time when there was a good trade in death, the Blums took over the things the neighbors used to do. The neighbors would help out when someone died, would see to the washing, dressing, and laying out of bodies. Now they were superseded by the undertaker's firm. Old customs that had seemed natural were now taboo. Touching the dead, bidding them farewell before they disappeared into their caskets. People were glad that now someone else would dispose of everything as quickly as possible, take the body away and stow it underground. A clean, matter-of-fact business.

The Blums were prominent figures in Innsbruck. They made a good living from the dead. First Hagen's father, then Hagen, now Blum. Just Blum, because she hated her first name, she'd never been able to bear it. *Brünhilde, leave the dead bodies in peace. Brün-hilde, stop playing with them. Brünhilde, stop sticking your fingers up their noses.* Brünhilde. A name that had nothing to do with her, a name they had given her because Hagen's name was more German than people liked these days, and because he wanted his daughter to fit into his world. A name that she had banished from her life. Only Blum now. No Brünhilde. Not since she was sixteen, not since she stopped being Hagen's little soldier, no longer did absolutely everything he told her to. Only Blum. She insisted on it. Never mind if he punished her for that.

She looks at the sky. She turns up the volume of the music, the boat rocks back and forth, there isn't a soul to be seen far and wide. No one to help them, no one to hear their screams. No one but her. She lies there naked, almost like a dead body in the preparation room. Bodies lying on the slab, cold and lifeless, for as long as she can remember. She didn't have any friends, the profession scared the other children off. They couldn't cope with the fact that her father's business was with the dead, and so was hers. Blum was a freak, and the other children laughed at her, excluded her from their games, mocked her and ganged up on her. She suffered all through her childhood and her teenage years. She longed for a friend, whether a boy or a girl, someone to share her life with, someone she could talk and laugh with. But she was all on her own, she had no one but her parents. Unloving parents. A silent mother who never hugged or kissed her, and a father who made her do things no child should ever have to do.

She'd been made to lay out the dead since she was seven. *There's no time to be lost, Brünhilde, the early bird catches the worm. Don't make such a fuss, Brünhilde, they're not going to bite you. Don't be so girly, Brünhilde, grit your teeth and stop crying. If you don't stop that noise this minute and do as I tell you, I'm going to put you in the casket, do you hear me, Brünhilde?* Blum shampooed the dead people's hair, she shaved them, she washed blood from their bodies and helped to dress them. She was ten years old when she first stitched up a mouth. Whenever she refused to perform a task, she was shut up in the casket. Countless times, for hours on end, a small, frightened child alone in the dark. She resisted, but Hagen broke her will every time. She was forced to lie in the casket while he screwed the lid down. *You leave me no alternative, Brünhilde. When are you going to stop fighting me? I really have no other option, Brünhilde.* And then the lid closed. A child in a wooden box. She held out as long as she could, she wished she could have been stronger, but she was only a child. She was helpless, she had to bear it, no one helped her, no one cared about her tears, her pleading. *I don't want to do it. I can't. Please don't make me do it.* That was just before she brought the needle up through the chin from below and into the mouth cavity, pulling the thread through dead flesh. She did everything, but it wasn't enough. Never mind how much she longed for a loving touch, to see her parents beam proudly. She was never good enough, however hard she tried. She was only a girl, defenseless and helpless, little Blum. *Please let me out, Papa. Please don't shut me up in there. Not in the casket again, Papa. Please don't.*

It was punishment and torment. Later on it was all in a day's work, but at first it was hell. She wiped out eyes and mouths a thousand times, cleaned blood and maggots away from wounds, touched cold, dead skin. There were disfigured corpses, severed body parts. It was no sort of childhood, she had no birthday cake, no candles, no dolls to dress and undress, only the dead. Big dolls, heavy dolls, hairy arms and legs, heads so heavy that she could hardly hold them, motionless mouths. Not a smile, not a kind word, nothing. Only her father driving her on. Through countless bodies, faces, genitals, and shit. A girl of ten wearing plastic gloves. Her mother would call her in for supper as if she had been playing with other little girls in the garden. *Supper's ready. Wash your hands. Don't keep Papa's favorite dinner waiting.* A nice roast for Papa, an accident victim for Blum. Hagen would put his loaded fork to his mouth. Blum would think of dead flesh, of old men with sores and papery skin, of the urine and blood in the room next door that she would have to mop up after supper. *This tastes delicious, Herta, a real poem of a dish, as always.* And Blum would push her plate away.

For as long as she can remember, there have been dead people around. They came in hearses, in ambulances, from autopsy tables; they came straight from their beds, where they had fallen asleep forever; they came with heart attacks, stabbed, or murdered; they simply came into Blum's life, invading her little world. No one asked her whether that was what she wanted. Whether she could cope with it. They were simply there, dead people sprawled on the aluminum table. It was terrifying at first, but after a while quiet and peaceful. Blum reconciled herself with her world, began to accept the fact that she had no choice, that there was nowhere else she could go. That it was the living she must fear, not the dead. That realization did her good. So did being alone with them. Whenever she could, she went into the preparation room. And in the end she made friends with the dead, she talked to them. Blum was stronger than they were. She could decide what happened to them. None of them could hurt her, never mind how big and heavy they were; they didn't move anymore. They didn't breathe, their arms and legs simply lay there. They were like dolls, big, cold dolls. She confided in them, she told them everything, and apart from that she kept quiet, not a word to her parents, she just did as she was told and then withdrew. Until now.

How the sun burns. The boat was always a respite from reality: a dream. From Trieste to Yugoslavia, to Greece, to Turkey, to Spain. Weeks on end on the boat, for weeks on end life was good. She looked forward to the time when the anchor was raised and the wind caught in the sails. When Hagen showed her the importance of the way you steered, and how to survive in a storm. Blum remembers all that she has learned and what she still has to learn, remembers the islands, the wind, and how her parents could even be induced to smile because they were on holiday. Their faces, usually so closed, opened up. Sometimes Blum even felt that she saw love in them, only briefly, a little flicker of love. For twenty years she has been looking for that, waiting for it, longing to be a normal girl, a daughter, a young woman capable of more than laying out bodies. She wants to live at last.

She is not going to move, never mind what happens, she isn't going to stir. There is nothing but Blum and the sun on her skin. She ignores the cries and the knocking on the hull.

Two desperate bodies, swimming. They can be seen from above. They try to get a handhold, their fingernails keep scraping along the side of the boat. The good old boat, the ladder that can be folded up, the ladder that isn't there when they shout for it. Hagen has insisted on keeping everything in its original condition, no renovations, no concessions to emergencies. *Don't get into a funk, only idiots forget the ladder up there, if that should ever happen to me you can leave me to drown.* How self-confident he was; how pitiful and helpless now. Big Hagen and his Herta. There's no way back for those two, they had simply jumped into the sea without thinking, two loveless old people. Two people with weak hearts, breathless, panicking. They've been screaming, they've been swallowing water for two hours now. They want to get back on board, they want to scale the side of the boat, they are trying everything, treading water, swimming beside the boat, weeping, screaming, drumming their fists on the wood, they call her name. *Brünhilde.* Again and again, *Brünhilde.* But Brünhilde doesn't hear them. Never mind how loud they scream, how badly their fingers are bleeding. She knows they will die. They know it too. They know that Blum can hear them, they know she's lying up here and doing nothing. Just listening to her music as the boat gently rocks. She smiles, knowing that soon it will be over. They'll stop screaming, and everything will finally be all right. Everything will be warm and almost happy. Only she and the sun, nothing else. She will come to life at last.

After three hours in the blazing sun, her skin is burning in silence. She can't hear a thing now, no more knocking on the side of the boat. Hagen and Herta silenced forever. Nothing is left, no past to which she must return. Blum will steer the boat now, bring it back to Trieste, she will renovate the house, build a new chapel of rest, a new preparation room, she will redevelop the whole place to the last nook and cranny. She'll throw away everything that reminds her of those two, take it to the trash dump. She is twenty-four years old. Now she'll stand up, get dressed, and radio the coast guard station, send a desperate message: her parents have disappeared without trace, just like that, while she was asleep. She will take a gulp of liquor from Hagen's flask and wait for help. She'll repeat her horror over the radio, she will scream and cry.

Forty minutes pass. Blum scans the sea for them while she waits. There is not a trace of Hagen. Or Herta. They simply disappeared in a tragic accident, two bodies with water in their lungs, washed ashore or fished out of the sea.

Blum stands on deck, waving. Shouting for help when she sees the boat. A small yacht, sailed by a tourist and not the coast guard, is the first to respond to her desperate cries. Blum, trembling, tells him what has happened. The stranger comes aboard to help her, looks after her, searches the boat and scrutinizes the sea around it. His voice does her good, consoles her, so do his arms as he puts them around her. Just like that, with sudden affection. His hands, the sunburn, her skin. *I went to sleep. It's my fault, we have to find them. Where are they, for God's sake, where can they be? What have I done? We must go back and search for them, they're not there anymore. They've gone, they've simply disappeared. What if they're dead?* She screams this out loud, tears herself away from him, strikes her own face again and again, blaming herself. *It's my fault,* she cries. When he tries to hold her she strikes him too, she weeps, she tries tearing herself away. She must do everything exactly right. Everything she says and does now must convince him, there must not be a moment's doubt in his mind. This attractive man. She lets him hold her, she is very close to him, her face on his chest, he holds her, she is breathing fast, she can smell him, she hears him. She hears his voice, whispering. *My name is Mark,* he says. *I'm a police officer. Everything will be all right.*

1

Uma jumps. Her little body flies through the air; there is a big smile on her face, she has small white teeth and happy eyes. A little girl of three; how cheerfully she lands and accepts the waiting embrace, snuggles close. *Mama, I had a dream about a bear, he growled so loud, he wanted to eat me up. I had to run away, Mama.* Blum hugs her, tenderly runs her fingers over the little head, touches the child's cheek and tells her that the bear only wanted to play, it was just a dream. *Nothing bad is going to happen; I'll look after you.* Blum's daughter Uma started talking a few months ago, she is an angel with blond curls. There's another angel too. Nela has gone back to sleep, lying contentedly in the crook of her father's arm. The children are in their parents' bed, first thing in the morning. It is a perfectly normal day for Blum and Mark.

Eight years ago, they touched each other for the first time. He put his arms around her on the boat. He was a wonderful man; right from the very first moment, he was there, taking care of her. Mark waited with her until the coast guard arrived, until she had answered hundreds of questions. He simply stayed by her side. Talking to the police officers on the case, he described how he had found Blum, assuring them that he did not doubt her version of the story. Everything went to show that she was telling the truth.

Her sunburn, her desperation, her tears: Blum had lost her parents in a tragic accident. And Mark had found her. A cop on holiday, a criminal investigation officer and an Austrian like Blum. A bachelor with a passion for sailing. It all fitted together, they had found one another, and to this day they haven't let each other go.

Their bodies are intertwined, skin against skin as they touch. They are very close, their mouths whisper *Good morning* before they begin playing with their children, growling playfully. Everything feels right. They lie happily beside each other, watching the little girls get out of bed and run off to visit their grandfather. *I want some cocoa, Papa. I want some salami, Mama. We're going to see Grandpa. You two are boring.* Blum laughs. Mark holds her lovingly in his arms, he won't let her go, she nestles close to him, purring. *I want to stay with you in this bed forever.* Blum enjoys every day, every hour of her whole life. His fingers have danced over her for eight years, they've been married for six, they have been a family for five. They plunged into their love passionately, and it still intoxicates them.

"Mark?"

"Yes?"

"Can't you just stay at home?"

"I'm afraid not, but I'll be back. There's a lot going on at the moment."

"Like what?"

"You don't want to know, my love."

"We could just pretend the world wasn't there."

"Well, yes, we could."

"But?"

"But I have to catch the villains."

"You don't have to. You want to."

"And you want to play with your dead people. I know you. You wouldn't last long here, in ten minutes' time you'd be jumping up and telling me there's something you have to do, the old lady brought in last night can't wait any longer."

"Would I?"

"Yes, you would."

"Two more minutes, okay?"

"Ten if you like."

Even on the boat, she had sensed that this man would make her happy. She knew from the way he held her and consoled her, even though he was a stranger. A criminal investigator in the police force, how absurd. He'd surely have been able to see through her, tear off her mask and get her imprisoned, he could have ended her new life before it had even begun. But it had turned out so differently. Blum wanted the embrace that had begun so suddenly never to end, she wanted to become acquainted with those arms, those hands. She wanted him, for the first time ever she wanted a man, for the first time she thought such a thing possible. She was ready to let him come close to her without hesitation or fear. Very close. And he wasn't deterred by her profession, he was not afraid of the dead.

She met him again. Back in the harbor in the Trieste, back in Austria. They understood one another and came together without many words. He was her friend, her protector, he was there when she buried her parents, he was there when she converted the Funerary Institute, he helped in any way he could. And after a while they shared their first kiss. They were sitting in the cool room, drinking beer, tired and happy. They had been retiling the preparation room, it was late summer, they were sweating and laughing as they sat on beer crates.

"Blum?"

"Yes?"

"This is the sexiest fridge I've ever sat in."

"Do you often sit in fridges?"

"Well, I'm a cop."

"So cops sit in fridges?"

"Of course."

"You're crazy."

"No crazier than you. I mean, it was your idea to have our first beer in here."

"This is our fourth beer."

"Stop counting, Blum."

"It really doesn't bother you that this place is normally filled with dead bodies?"

"No."

"I spent a lot of time in this room when I was a child."

"With the bodies or without them?"

"With them."

"Doors open or closed?"

"Closed."

"Why?"

"It was my hiding place. They didn't come looking for me, so I often spent hours in here. I just sat and watched the dead."

"Pretty cold, wasn't it, with the door closed?"

"Not in long underwear, a ski suit, gloves, and a hat."

"Sounds a bit crazy, but I believe you."

"You should."

"You wouldn't lie to me, would you?"

"What do you mean?"

"You're honest with me."

"Why wouldn't I be?"

"Can I trust you?"

"Why do you ask that?"

"Because I have to kiss you."

"Do you?"

"I can't help it, I've been wanting to for the last two months. I really wanted to when I saw you on the boat. I'm sorry, I really need to."

"So you have to trust me to kiss me?"

"If I kiss you, I'll want to marry you. And then it's surely a good thing to trust each other, don't you think?"

"But you don't know me."

"Yes, I do."

"When I was little I played with dead bodies."

"And I put cats in a sack and drowned them. I put fireworks in frogs and watched them explode."

"No, you didn't."

"I did."

"Why?"

"I was curious."

"Me too."

"And that's why I have to kiss you."

"Don't I get any say in it?"

"Certainly not."

How lovely it was. How close their faces came, their lips. How their mouths met, soft, excited, trembling. Familiar and strange and lovely. Blum and Mark in the cool room. To this day their mouths have gone on touching.

It was a two-story Jugendstil villa in the middle of Innsbruck, with a large backyard with apple trees. When Hagen and Herta were underground Blum tore everything old out of the house: her parents' bedroom, the old pine-paneled living room, the kitchen. Nothing was left except the old wooden floor; she kept that and sanded it down. The work took her hours. She scrubbed and painted, and Mark helped her. He offered to, and she thanked him. *If you don't have anything better to do. How can anyone be so friendly and kind? Are you really sure you don't have a girlfriend?* He said no, frowning, and Blum relished it all: the fact that he kept coming back, that he had decided to take care of her. That he thought she was beautiful, and took days off for her. That he even brought his colleagues to lend a hand. Half the province's police officers helped them to tear down the walls and clear the rubble.

The Blums' house was gutted and refurbished, the walls were painted in new, bright colors, and the old ghosts were banished. Together with Mark, she wandered all through the house at night, smoking them out. She and Mark went from room to room, and smoke rose; the scent of juniper, cinnamon, and orange peel lingered in the air. Whether Mark believed in it or not, he went with her, helping the witch with her exorcism, making an effort to feel the evil within the walls. They went from cellar to attic, flooding every corner with positive thoughts, and all that had been there before disappeared. Blum threw all thoughts of Hagen and Herta, of her old life with them, out with the trash. What was left was a dream house, an oasis of peace in the middle of Innsbruck, a modern Funerary Institute in the shade of the apple trees, managed by a young woman who treated both the dead and the mourners with respect. The business began to flourish. Like Blum herself.

After the kiss in the cool room, Mark moved in with her. Love suddenly filled the old villa. It was all like a dream, a fairy tale come true, just like in the books that Blum had read, the stories in which she had taken refuge. It was the happiness of others that had kept her alive, and her own longing for it. Something she had never really believed in now lies beside her. She wants everything to stay as it is, nothing to change. She says so every day, every day she asks him not to stop loving her. A kiss before they begin each new day, and then, thankful for it, she moves away from him and jumps out of bed. In the old days Blum would never for a moment have thought that happiness could fill her like this. That she would be granted little human beings and would love them. Back then she didn't like to think of what would happen next, she simply flung herself into Mark's embrace. She hadn't dared to think of children. She was afraid the happiness would go away if she asked too much of it, that love would disappear overnight. Having her own children, seeing them grow up, loving them—for three years Blum dismissed the idea from her mind. She couldn't imagine being a mother, she was afraid of repeating what she had learned. Lovelessness, coldness of heart, she didn't want to find out whether she was another Herta or Hagen. When Mark broached the idea, fear constricted her throat, kept her quiet. She didn't dare to try for them, not for a long time, but in the end she overcame her fears. Her wish for children was too great. But she was granted her wish twice. They were miraculous little creatures. Blum worried over every tear they shed, every fit of crying, she took care of them and touched them whenever she could, she carried them around for hours, caressed them, spoke lovingly to them. She lay awake at night looking at her angels as they slept. To this day she sometimes doubts that it can be true, that they are really here.

2

Uma and Nela are upstairs with Karl, Mark's father, who is sitting reading the morning paper when the girls storm into his kitchen. He is a kind old man who makes hot chocolate for the children, laughs with them, helps them to play with their building blocks, who loves them and would do anything for them. Uma is in the crook of his arm, Nela is spooning up hot chocolate from a pink cup. Karl tells them stories over breakfast; he is a blessing to everyone in the house. Mark and Blum brought him to live with them two years ago. He had suffered an infection from a tick bite, and then took early retirement after a stroke. He now needs help in many situations—he would never ask for that help, but he is glad of it. There are things that he forgets these days, things he can no longer remember. Mark didn't want to leave him on his own in his little apartment, and so Blum suggested converting the unused second story of the house. Knowing how much he meant to Mark, she wanted Karl to live with them. For a long time he had done everything for his son. Mark's mother died young, and Karl was the only parent he could remember. When Mark woke up, when he went to sleep, Karl and only Karl was there. Karl brought the boy up on his own: two men at the breakfast table, fatherly advice when he had a spare moment. They stuck together as much as they could. Mark spent a good deal of time on his own, a little boy under the covers, but a little boy who could always trust his father to come back. Who knew that nothing bad would happen to him, that the bond between them was stronger than anything else. Mark was a loner; as a teenager he knocked around like a stray dog, but he was happy, as happy as possible, because of all the trouble that Karl took. He told Blum about his life as a motherless adolescent, about those frequent father-and-son chats in the kitchen. Karl would sit at the table with his evening glass of beer while Mark washed the dishes.

"Do you know what you want to do, Mark? After school, I mean?"

"I'm going to join the police. Same as you. The criminal investigation department."

"You don't know what you're talking about, boy."

"Yes, I do."

"It's not always a pleasant job."

"What job is?"

"We went to pick up a young mother at her apartment today. She'd shaken her baby to death. Her sister found them and called us. The mother was sitting on the floor cradling the baby; she cried when the paramedics took the child out of her arms. She said the baby wouldn't stop crying. She just wanted peace."

"We're out of dishwashing liquid."

"Did you understand what I was saying, Mark?"

"That's life, Papa."

"No, it isn't, or it is only for people like me who decide to earn their living that way. You don't have to see things like that, you can avoid it."

"But I don't want to."

"You should go to college, Mark, and then the whole world's your oyster, you can always join the police later."

"But I want to join right away."

"Why?"

"If it's good enough for you, then it's good enough for me."

"I know your mother would have wanted you to go to college and study. Economics or medicine."

"But my mother isn't here."

"I know."

"You really don't have to worry about me."

"I'm so sorry, Mark."

"What for?"

"Everything."

"You did everything right by me, everything, don't you understand that? So now drink that beer and stop worrying."

Twenty years later Karl is telling the children stories. Uma and Nela love him: his beard—they rub their smooth skin against it—his voice, his arms tossing them up in the air, his laughter. Karl's life is a simple one now. There are no more crimes, no more corpses, only the children and the armchair where he spends his days. He sits in it, listening to music for hours on end or sits out on the terrace, holding his face up to the sun. Mark always keeps an eye on his father, covers him up when he has fallen asleep in his chair. The children love him; their parents can see it in their faces when they come down from the top floor and repeat the stories that Grandpa has told them.

The past is forgotten, Blum's life before Mark. She sits at the breakfast table, smiling at the way Mark holds out his coffee cup, looking at her. Smiling as she spreads honey on her bread, tells the children how bees make honey, tells them not to dawdle, they have to go to school. She is impatient but still loving as she hurries them up, asking all the same if they want another slice of bread and honey.

Watching them munch and smack their lips, spreading honey all over the table, while she talks to Mark.

"When will you be home today?"

"Late."

"Difficult case?"

"Yes."

"What is it?"

"You don't want to know, Blum."

"Maybe I do."

"The world's a bad place; it's enough for me to have to deal with it."

"My hero, my rescuer, the good conscience of the city!"

"There's something strange going on here."

"Do you want to talk about it?"

"No."

"You can, you know. I can handle it."

"Yes, but all the same no. I have to be certain first. Right now I'm on my own with it. I could be seeing a crime where there isn't one."

"Trust your instinct."

"That's the problem, because that's exactly what I am doing."

"You'll get the guilty behind bars and make sure that justice is done. And I'll see to the old man who's been brought to the Institute."

"How did he die?"

"You don't want to know."

"Maybe I do."

All is well, there's no rage, no anger, no sadness, nothing like that. Nothing hurts, the clients aren't getting on her nerves this morning, the children are behaving. There's nothing to worry her; it's a good day. Blum enjoys this untroubled feeling, her happiness when she looks at Mark. The corners of his mouth turning up, the peace radiating from him, his strength. She feels safe, protected. Mark is her home, he is there and he won't go away. Never mind how loud she shouts, never mind if she gets angry, never mind whether she sometimes has doubts about life and fears it. Mark will be lying beside her when she wakes. She can sense him there, always.

Blum knows there is something troubling him, some cause for anxiety. It is gnawing away at him, silently and secretly, but Blum notices it. However hard he tries to leave his job behind when he comes home in the evening, he doesn't always succeed. Blum can see that his thoughts are racing, that he can't let something go. Something keeps taking his attention away from her and the children. Mark the policeman and his passion for his job. If anyone asks him what he does, he talks about it with enthusiasm. He says that there could be no better career in the world for him, nothing could stop him from believing in justice. He loves what he does, he believes in it, and he is also ready to throw away the rule book now and then to achieve his aims. Mark believes in his instincts, and indeed he feels more than he thinks; logic isn't always his strong point. He follows his gut, trusts his nose, follows up after a remark, an impression. He believes in intuition, and he believes everything his father has taught him, all the little details that he has observed over the years, discussing his father's assessment of a situation over his evening beer. Their long conversations about unsolved cases, even before Mark had really made up his mind to join the police. Karl was his teacher; he taught him how to be human. He might have smiled at the idea of instinct when he was sixteen, but he took it to heart, and he does to this day. *Sometimes you have to make decisions, Mark, and never mind what other people say, you will have to do as your heart tells you. No violence, no infringement of the law.*

Don't kick a man when he is down. You're on the side of the angels and you must never forget it. Karl made Mark a police officer, one of the best. And one who sometimes lets pity take precedence over the law. Mark always tries to discover the reason for a crime; he wants to know how it came to pass, why someone comes to be guilty of an offense. Why they will risk contempt and imprisonment. Why a man is prepared to attack an ATM with a sledgehammer. A man like Reza.

3

It was six years ago. Reza was simply after the money, or some of it, just enough to survive on. He was hungry and wanted to buy food. He had put the CCTV camera on the facade of the building out of action with a stone, and covered the camera in the cash dispenser with sticky tape. When Mark came along he was hitting the dispenser for the umpteenth time. With all his might, again and again, bringing the sledgehammer down where the cash would be. Reza never noticed Mark charging at him. Mark forced him back. It was like the war: a soldier on the ground, injured, desperate, the enemy above him with a gun in his hand. Mark was aiming it at Reza as he made him lie flat on his front and surrender.

Reza is a Bosnian, and for the last six years he has been working as an undertaker. He is Blum's assistant, her right-hand man. He lost everything in the war, his brothers, his parents, his house. Everything burnt down; not a trace remained. The fact that he survived was nothing short of miraculous; he had hidden, had watched the Serbs slaughtering his countrymen. Overnight, he had to learn what war meant, how brutal life could be, how bloody and raucous death was. He had nothing now, no one who was there for him or cared for him, no roof over his head, no money, nothing. Nothing but blood and war and killing. He had often simply struck out on his own. It had been easy. Even before he was eighteen he had killed people in the war to survive. The memories came flooding back. Reza talked half the night through, laying out his life before their eyes. Mark and Blum listened, openmouthed, as they heard what he had to say: incredible stories of a child toting a gun.

Mark had been on his way home. It was pure chance that he saw the man with the sledgehammer at all. A brief glance to his right changed everything, and Reza's life took a sudden turn for the better. Instead of ending up in prison, he was in Mark and Blum's villa. Instead of being kicked and humiliated, he was given food and a roof over his head. No one had seen them, no cameras, no passersby. Nothing had been stolen; the only harm done was some damage to the cash dispenser. Mark had made his decision; he thought he was doing the right thing. The man on the ground represented no threat, and locking him up was no solution, so he took Reza home with him. He and Blum took the homeless Bosnian in, for the time being. At that time, no one guessed that he would stay for years. Blum made chicken soup, they sat at the kitchen table and listened to his story. *Thank you*, he kept saying, over and over again, *thank you*. Blum didn't hesitate for a moment. Mark had decided to help him, and she did what Mark wanted. She was looking for a new employee at the time, which probably had as much influence on her decision as the fact that Reza was not afraid of death. It had been an everyday occurrence for so long he did not fear the corpses on the preparation table. Everything came together. They extended the workshop under the Institute building to make it into living quarters for Reza. He had arrived.

Reza is standing in the garden, washing the hearse. He has been Blum's devoted assistant for the past six years. Reza has improved everyone's life; the clients, Karl, and the children all like him. To

Uma and Nela, Reza has always been there. The man with the funny accent is part of the family. He tosses them up in the air in summer, catches them as they come down, and smiles. Now Reza is carefully polishing the hearse. Mark is getting on his motorcycle, Karl will take the girls to school, and Blum and Reza will finally attend to the old man lying in the cool room.

Blum is curious; she hasn't seen the body yet, all she knows is that it was a gunshot to the head, the suicide of an eighty-four-year-old man who no longer wanted to live, who put an end to it all with a bullet. Reza and another driver collected him from the forensic lab yesterday. Blum is interested to know what his head looks like, how large a hole the bullet made. Only a little kiss stands between her and her next adventure, a kiss for Mark. *I love you*, he says again. Then he rides away.

Blum watches him go. Everything follows its normal course; the engine snarls as the man she loves sets off for his day's work. When he has driven twenty meters, he switches on the turn signal and turns back once, briefly, to look at Blum and Reza, then he twists the right-hand throttle and accelerates. Blum is just about to go back into the house when she hears the bang.

She sees it, a Rover, a large black car. At first she can't work out what is happening, she doesn't understand. The car. The way Mark disappears. The way the big car pushes him aside, knocks him over. The way he falls, and the car drives over him. Reza beginning to run, with Blum in pursuit. Mark disappearing under the car, the loud sound of metal as the motorcycle is dragged along. Mark's body turns like a puppet, flies through the air like a toy. She runs to him, she wants to help, Reza tries to hold her back. And the car simply drives away, fast and forever. Without stopping to help, without expressing regret or horror. Just the back of a car driving away from an accident, from a motorcycle lying smashed on the asphalt, from a lifeless body. He lies there, he doesn't move. There is no sound. There's nothing anymore. All that was loud is silent again, as if nothing has happened. A fine day is beginning, the sun is shining. Mark lies in her arms. Blum screams. Long and loud.

For minutes on end her voice rises above the road. She pleads, she begs, her mouth opens and closes. Her upper body rocks forward, rocks back, Mark's head is in her lap, blood everywhere. Tears everywhere, running down her cheeks, splashing him, wanting him to move, to breathe, to say something. She has taken off his helmet, she holds his face in her hands, she looks at him, looks into his empty eyes, she howls, she whimpers, she strokes his hair again and again with the palm of her hand. Everything is blood, everything is broken, nothing is whole anymore.

Reza calls the emergency numbers, an ambulance, the police. He is running around in circles like a frightened animal, he doesn't know what to do, how to help, there is no way out. Staring neighbors, horrified faces, no one can help. No one can bring Mark back. Five minutes ago everything was all right, five minutes ago there was still life, and now there's only death. It has knocked everything over and crushed it. Blum knows that there is no going back now. That he will never touch her again, that his fingers will be silent, his hands, his mouth. She knows this. She has seen death a thousand times, she has seen life departed, only a body, only skin going cold. There will be no more talk, no laughing, no one to protect her anymore. Mark will not come back. Blum knows it, senses it, feels it. Feels it tearing at her heart, feels everything in her cut to pieces as she screams and screams because the pain is growing worse every second.

Blum and Mark are in the middle of the road. The motorcycle lies fifty meters away. Blum hears the children screaming too, they are crying. Blum sees Karl and Reza holding them back. They want to go to their father, they want to go to Blum, they can hear their mother. They hear how desperate she is. Police officers climb out of their car and paramedics drag her away. Blum's fingers touch Mark one last time. The needle goes into her arm. They hold her, they press her down to the ground, she screams. Until suddenly it is warm, and the light goes out.

4

She has slept for thirty-six hours. Again and again she was briefly awoken, again and again she forced her eyes to close. She didn't want to come back to the light of day, to reality, didn't want to feel anything, see anything, accept that it had really happened. Her sole wish was to sleep, immersing herself in the fog that made everything bearable. Blum turns over and goes back to sleep. She never wants to wake again. She wants to numb herself for days on end, for weeks. Not until Uma and Nela crawl into bed with her and little hands begin stroking her cheek does she come back.

She senses the fear and desperation in their small fingers. She hears her children's consoling words; they are trying to be strong, they want their mother back, they want her to get up and go on living. *Mama, you mustn't be dead. Please get up, Mama. You must open your eyes, Mama. Please.* Nela's voice. She wants to be cuddled, she wants Blum to dry her tears, she wants to be told that everything is all right. Those two magical little creatures don't understand why their papa isn't there or why he was covered with blood or why he was taken away. They don't want their world to collapse; they want to snuggle up to their mother, crawl into her, hide in her, be safe. They want to act as if everything were still the same. As if Mark were still there beside them. Breathing, smiling. *Mama, you must get up now. Please, you must. Grandpa won't stop crying. We need you, Mama.* Their words sink far down into Blum. Their words tear Blum away from sleep and suddenly give her strength. She can't lie here for another moment. With all her might, she sits up and comes back to life. *I'm not dead,* she says.

"We'll manage, my big girl."

"What, Mama? What will we manage?"

"Come here, you two."

"What's the matter with Papa, Mama? I want him to come back."

"Papa won't be coming back."

"Why not?"

"Nela, don't you know that Papa is a prince?"

"So?"

"So princes ride through the forest fighting dragons."

"Dragons aren't real, Mama."

"Oh yes, Nela, there are dragons, and your papa has gone away to fight them. Your papa is a very brave prince."

"Why was there all that blood, Mama?"

"That was dragon's blood. The dragon wounded your papa, but he's better again now. Now he is riding through the forest on his white horse."

"You're telling stories, Mama."

"Imagine it, Nela, think of him smiling as he rides."

"Papa doesn't have a horse, he has a motorcycle. And the motor-cycle is broken. It was lying in the road. Just like Papa."

"Your Papa is all right."

"Papa is dead."

"No."

"Yes, Mama. Papa is a corpse now too."

"Hush."

"They've just brought him back."

"What are you talking about?"

"Papa is in the cool room."

Blum jumps up. Nela's words are like ice-cold water into which she is falling, nearly drowning, while her heart almost stops because it hurts so much, because everything is suddenly real again. Because the idea that the children have seen their dead father is like a blow to the face. It mustn't be real. Not like that, not before she has done what needs doing. She must get up, she must think clearly, she must see to everything, bring the sinking ship back on course. Where is Karl? Where's Reza? Why does everything hurt so much?

Mark. She is screaming inside, she is weeping, pleading. *Come back, please. I need you. I can't do it without you. I can't. The children. How am I to do it without you? I don't know. Please, Mark. Look at them. They're so small. Look at them clinging to me. I can't do it, Mark. I can't do it without you.* But all the same she gets dressed and goes into the kitchen with the children. All the same, she opens the fridge and makes them something to eat. All the same, she acts as if she has everything back under control. Never mind how loudly she is screaming inside, never mind if everything in her is collapsing; every piece of skin crying out, every inch of flesh. It hurts as if she were being torn apart by a herd of wild beasts. But she spreads butter on her toast and even tries to smile, to soothe the children's fears. She mustn't cry now. Mustn't lie there motionless and desperate, never to stand up again, as if she were dead.

They are sitting side by side at the table. The children are munching away; Blum watches them. Everything will be all right, she says, knowing that's not true. Nothing will ever be all right again. Everything that was once all right is now lying in a cool room on the ground floor. He will never read the children a story again, never

35

play with them again, never make them another bonfire in the backyard. No more singing together, no more suppers together, no more outings, no vacations on the boat. The children were so happy when he put their life jackets on. In her mind's eye Blum sees them on the loveliest beaches in Croatia, a month ago. They ran into the water, he tossed them up in the air, they were so happy, and nothing threatened their little world, Mama and Papa were there, and when they went to sleep Mama and Papa sat out on the deck, drinking wine. She heard their voices, their giggling, there was such confidence that no storm in the world could make their boat capsize. Love was there, everything was all right. By night on the sea.

"Do you still want more?"

"Lots more."

"My lady, you need to get your sea legs."

"I'm on vacation."

"You're drunk, my love."

"And?"

"And nothing."

"Well, there we are."

"I'm afraid you may molest me again tonight."

"You're right, but not just yet. There's half a bottle left to go."

"Drink up quickly, my lady."

"There's no hurry, my good sir."

"Hurry up, the stars will soon be setting."

"No, they won't."

"They will."

"Then I suppose I really ought to drink more quickly."

"We don't want to lose any time."

"Do the stars just fall out of the sky, or what?"

"Yes, they all fall into the sea, just like that. They dive into the water and disappear. One after another. Until the sky is empty."

"I'd like to see that."

"It's a beautiful sight, Blum."

"That's what you are."

"What?"

"A beautiful sight."

"Mhmm . . . Do you think you'll ever tire of this? You've been sailing in these waters for twenty-five years."

"They're my home."

"Home?"

"I was always happy here."

"Until the day I found you."

"How do you mean?"

"That was a very sad time."

"Do we have to talk about it now?"

"I'm sorry. Forget it, Blum."

"I wish it was as easy as that."

"I can kiss you."

"Will that help?"

"I'm sure it will."

"My happiness began the day you came on board the boat. Before that, I wasn't really happy except in summer. There was one season, not four. No autumn, no winter, no spring. Just a couple of weeks in summer."

"Lovely."

"What's lovely?"

"You. Everything. You're like a poem."

"I'm drunk, don't you forget."

"You're like a beautiful turn of phrase."

"A turn of phrase?"

"A beautiful turn of phrase that intoxicates you and never lets you go. Not a word too many, simple and clear."

"Like what?"

"The sky has been turning slowly."

"Doing what?"

"The sky has been turning slowly."

"You're crazy."

"But it's beautiful, right?"

"Mark, darling Mark, my romantic cop. First the stars fall out of the sky, and then the sky itself is turning."

"That's exactly it. And all just for you."

Somewhere off Zadar, they were naked on deck, entwined with one another, the sea as smooth as a mirror, and as silent. The sea was their home. But now their lives have been switched off, there is no sound of waves breaking, no blue sky. Mark will never see it again. Nothing is left but the munching of the children, their sad eyes, the silent kitchen. Blum forces the images of the sea back into her mind the way she wants to remember them; she wants to go back to yesterday, back to the boat, back to his warm skin. That's where she wants to be. She can't get there. She has to hug her children, play with them, read to them, she has to look after them. Until their little eyes close, until night rescues her. Then she will go to those images. Then, not now.

5

She looks at his ruined body, his injured skin. They have cut him open and sewn him up again, they have opened up his head, they've tested his blood and internal organs to ascertain whether he was under the influence of drink or drugs; they wanted to make sure that he was not to blame. After her collapse, he had been taken to the forensics lab. No one wanted to make a mistake. It was up to the investigators and the public prosecutor to decide whether there should be an autopsy in the case of a hit-and-run, and the public prosecutor had decided to cut his skull open, remove his brain, open his rib cage like a shopping bag, and stitch it up again. They have left him looking worse than before, even more wounded.

Blum wants to be alone with him. She has asked Reza to leave them. She doesn't know what will happen, whether she will weep and scream. She doesn't know anything anymore, except that her husband is lying motionless in front of her, naked and dead. Like all the others she has tended to over the past twenty years. Corpses, lifeless bodies with open mouths, torn away from life. But she has never had to shed tears, never felt pain and grief, never. Death is an everyday thing for Blum, it doesn't frighten her, or at least it didn't until now. This time is different. Entirely different. Everything she's ever seen in her life is a joke, ridiculous compared with what lies before her now.

All she can do is stand there, surveying his torn, hollowed corpse. She can't cry yet. The dried blood, his face that, as if by miracle, has been preserved intact. Blum's eyes move over his body; it is all familiar to her. She has kissed every inch of his skin. She loves every inch of him so much that she doesn't know whether she can go on living without him. She stands there, looking, breathing, swallowing. She wants to die so much, simply to be done with it all, to feel nothing anymore. She doesn't want to be reminded that life was once good, that she was happy. Blum feels like bashing her head against the wall, smashing it a hundred times against the white tiles, she wants the pain to stop, she wants the knife in her breast to stop burrowing and digging and cutting. She wants to be dead like him.

She works in her usual way, as if operated by remote control. All of a sudden she sets to work preparing him, rubbing the blood away from his skin with cotton wool and albumin solution, she cleans his injuries, lovingly treating them all. Her hands do not tremble as she stitches up his wounds, she tries to reconstruct everything; she opens the stitches on his head, removes clotted blood, and care-fully stitches the cut up again. She puts him back in order as best she can. She fills deep wounds with cellulose, restores the distorted parts of his body to their proper shape, washes his hair and blows it dry. She shaves him. Blum goes about her work. For a split second she even forgets that it is Mark lying there, that it is his mouth she is closing forever, exactly as Hagen taught her. She inserts a curved needle into a fold of skin behind his chin, runs it through the soft palate, brings it up below the right-hand side of his upper lip and into his right nostril, and out again into a small fold of skin by his septum. Then she puts the needle through the septum into the left nostril, and takes it back in the opposite direction, through the left half of his upper lip and down. She stitches his mouth up, a mandible ligature, just as she has learned to do. It is the most natural thing in the world for her to run the needle back through his chin, pulling the jaw shut with the ends of the thread and tying the knot, forming his lips into a smile. She stares at those lips, and begins to cry. Her tears collect on his skin. Then she forces herself to go on and bandage his head to hide the wounds. Next his clothes. With great effort, she gets him dressed. His body is heavy, but even without Reza's help she rolls him onto his side. His broken legs. His favorite trousers, his white T-shirt.

Blum climbs up on the preparation table and lies down beside him. She can't help it, just one more time. She will lie beside him, hold his hand, feel him very close before he disappears underground. Only briefly, no one will see. Reza won't come back, Karl will not come into the preparation room either, they are alone. Two bodies fitted snugly on the narrow table. Blum's fingers are entwined with his, but they don't move, however hard she squeezes them. However much she wishes they would, there's no movement, only his cold skin, something like closeness this one last time, a memory of times past before she puts him in the casket. Before they come to see him for the last time: Reza, Karl, their friends, the children. They will say good-bye to him tomorrow, everything will take its familiar course, the body on show, the blessing, the burial. They will lower him into the grave and shovel earth into it, he will decompose in an oak casket, be eaten by worms. Soon there will be nothing left but the bones, and later not even those. But now his hand is still in hers. She can still touch him, feel him, he is lying beside her, his body, his face. He is still there, just for a night, only for a few hours. So she stays where she is. She makes no sound, tries not to breathe, she holds her breath, desperately trying to catch some sound, some small sign that he is still alive, only asleep. But there's nothing apart from her breathing, the rise and fall of her rib cage. Only Blum and her dead husband. Only her thoughts, her pain, her rage, her despair, her own heart burning, crying out. Blum and Mark. Mark eradicated, just like that.

6

Massimo is weeping. His wife stands beside him, and Karl next to them. Blum and the children are standing beside the grave, right at the front, throwing sunflowers into its depths. The yellow petals lie on the casket, a comforting image but just for a moment. Flowers for Papa. The sight of the flowers hurts; the hurt is even greater than it was at first, now, after three days without him. Three days in which they have been searching desperately for their ordinary lives. Reza was at the helm, organizing everything. He was there for Blum, for the children, for Karl. But for him the boat would have capsized. He is strong, he doesn't shed tears, but his smile has disappeared, the smile that had come to his face years ago when his life at the villa began.

Reza helped to carry the casket; he coordinated everything, drew up the death announcement, organized the funeral. Blum didn't have to worry about anything because Reza was in charge, she could devote herself to the children, to taking their minds off sad subjects, preparing them, explaining step by step what would happen. Trying to tell them that the casket will simply disappear into the ground. That death is a part of life and takes what it wants, like a wild beast tearing apart a sheep. A car coming out of nowhere.

Sunflowers falling. She put it in prettier, less truthful terms, not wanting to frighten the children, wishing to spare them.

The sun is shining in the cemetery. Reza looks after Karl, supporting the old man. Karl can hardly stand, his legs won't carry him, he hasn't been able to eat or sleep. He has aged several years in these three days. Many of the mourners are weeping, the police band plays a funeral march, countless colleagues of Mark's are present, and Massimo, Mark's best friend, delivers the eulogy. He remembers the good times, the operations they undertook together. Mark was one of the good cops, says Massimo, a man with a heart, unforgettable, a loss to all who knew him. Massimo sheds more tears.

One by one they throw earth down into the grave. Then the mourners leave him alone. Mark is deep down in the ground, in his casket. He is on his own, while they all go to the restaurant and drink to him. They offer Blum help and condolences, they assure her that things will get better. She can hardly look them in the eye; they are as powerless as she is. Helplessly, she sits with a bowl of chicken soup; helplessly, she tries to persuade the children to eat. There's no more that she can do. She can only be there for them, love them, give them all she has. She mustn't leave them alone with their pain and their fear; the children are all she has left of him. How sad they are, and how strong. They endure what has happened, are adjusting to it. They sit still and wait for the storm to pass. Blum strokes their hair, Uma's hair, Nela's hair. And Massimo takes Blum aside, puts his arm round her affectionately.

"Drink this."
"No."
"Go on, have a drink."

"If you insist."

"I'm so sorry, Blum."

"I know."

"And you know that I'll always be there for you."

"But even you can't bring him back, can you?"

"No, I can't do that. Mark was one of the most important people in my life too; I owe him this."

"You owe him what?"

"Taking care of you for him."

"No one has to take care of me."

"Yes, they do, Blum. Ute and I can help you with the children."

"That won't be necessary."

"You'll need all the help you can get, Blum. Don't be so stubborn, I mean you well. You know how much I care about you and the children."

"You have enough problems of your own."

"They're not important now."

"Mark said you're getting a divorce."

"Let's not discuss that here, please, Blum."

"Why not? Let's talk about your failed marriage; let's talk about your wife and her little problem."

"Why are you doing this, Blum?"

"What am I doing? Look at her, she's babbling, she can hardly stand up straight. And it's only midday. Maybe you'd do better to take care of Ute, not me."

"Maybe I should leave you alone."

"Maybe you should."

"Anything you say. I'll go."

"Oh no."

"What do you mean, no?"

"Please stay. I'm sorry I spoke like that, Massimo. I didn't mean it."

"That's all right."

"I don't know if I can manage without him. With the children, with everything. I just don't know."

"You have Reza and Karl. You have me."

"I wish I could die. Don't you understand that? I wish I could die."

"You don't, Blum. You're strong, you'll survive even without him."

Massimo passes his right hand over her back, up and down. It's the only thing he can do, the only thing that helps. Words are no use; Blum doesn't want to hear them. She doesn't want to think, to envisage the future. She just wants it to be night, for the lights to go out so sleep can come. She doesn't want to think, or feel anything but Massimo's hand going up and down her back.

7

Two weeks have passed, two weeks without him. It is still summer, the children run round the garden in short dresses. Karl is sitting in his armchair while Blum hangs out washing. It is almost as if everything were all right again; from the outside looking in, life is the same. The backyard, the old apple trees, the swing going back and forth, Uma flooding the flower bed in the garden, Nela rubbing dirt into a doll's hair. The sky stands still, not a cloud in sight. It still hurts. When she wakes up, when she goes to sleep, when the children talk about him. Blum knows it won't get any better, it won't stop eating away at her, but she has decided not to die, not to drop by the wayside. Instead, she will get up every morning and go on living for the children. Never mind how difficult it is, she must stay here, go on, put one foot in front of the other however heavy her legs feel. And never mind how much she longs to deaden her memories with pills and alcohol. She has to decide against Valium and vodka every evening once the children are in bed. She must be in working order, although she wants only to forget. Every morning she tries yet again to be cold and invulnerable. And every morning she fails.

There's still no sign of the hit-and-run car. The driver can't be traced and seems to have disappeared from the face of the earth.

He was probably drunk, driving too fast, but he must have seen Mark. The police have no clues, there's no black Rover in the local garages, they've followed up on all leads. *Hit-and-run, outcome fatal*, say the files, *driver unknown*. A driver who got away with his life and his liberty, snuffing out Mark's just like that. He could have been on his phone, typing an e-mail, sending a text, maybe he just nodded off. Blum will never know. They'll never find him, although Massimo is doing his best.

He's been good to his word and been there for her ever since the funeral, helping her to wind up Mark's official life, visiting offices, insurance firms, lawyers, notaries. Massimo shields her from everyday life, and Reza does too. So that she can look after the children, so that she can survive, so that the tears don't drown her. The business is running as usual because people don't stop dying. Reza collects the dead from care homes, from the forest, from their offices, their beds, the street; he does his job the way Blum taught him. He works the whole time, he says little, his feelings are hidden somewhere obscure. He has fewer words than Massimo, in fact none at all. So he is glad that Massimo is looking after Blum, acting as a buffer for her, listening to her pain.

Massimo is a friend of many years' standing, Mark's colleague and indeed his superior officer. He is only three years older than Mark but rose quickly in the ranks. Massimo spends more time at the police station than at home. Because he loves his job, he says. Because he doesn't want to be at home, Mark used to say. His marriage is over; Ute has taken up the bottle. The children they'd wanted never came along. They tried for years. He and Ute saw Blum having babies without any difficulty. Their friends' happiness highlighted their own failure. Much as she wanted to, Ute never got pregnant, and even IVF didn't work. Their unhappiness grew worse, their desperate longing was a heavy burden on their marriage. So heavy indeed that Ute began drinking. Massimo suffers from it more every month; his friends see the unhappiness to which he wakes every morning written on his face. None of his attempts to help Ute have come to anything. He tried persuading her to go to therapy, said he would go to marriage counseling with her. Nothing worked; she wouldn't let anyone or anything come near her. Blum realizes that he is suffering more than he admits. She can see that he has already given Ute up as a hopeless case, and no longer wanted to intervene when she climbed up on the table at the funeral, blind drunk. That was two weeks ago, and he was slow to go to her aid. Trying to restrain Ute was nothing but his duty, and all that he could manage was damage control. Shaking his head, embarrassed to know that everyone in the room was staring and pitying him, because Ute had lost control, was screaming and shouting, *Isn't there some bastard around here who can give me a fucking child? Come along, get your damn dick out and fuck me, why don't you?* Ute was scrambling over the tables, screaming. Massimo eventually followed, seized her, and dragged her outside.

Such marital dramas occur almost daily. Massimo is taking every opportunity to avoid his wife and come to help Blum instead. She gets all that he still has to give, and she is grateful not to be alone, to have someone other than Reza and Karl for company. Someone to put his arms round her. She is glad when his car turns into the drive, when he hugs the children, fools around with them for a moment in the backyard, tries to make them laugh. Massimo is a friend—one of the good cops, like Karl and Mark. He disappears into the house with a smile, and comes back with a bottle of white wine and two glasses. Things are all in order, he tells her.

She is financially secure; Mark had taken out life insurance. There's nothing for her to worry about, he says, opening the bottle and pouring the wine. Money for Mark's death, thinks Blum. A lot of money. *What a fucking awful world*, she says, drinking her wine in long, thirsty gulps.

8

The children are asleep. Massimo has gone; he put the girls to bed, read them a story, and left, although he would have liked to stay and talk to Blum a little longer. She wanted to be alone in Mark's study, sitting in his armchair, legs up on the desk, just as Mark himself used to sit drinking wine in the earthenware goblets they had brought back from Greece; they liked drinking from those rather than from more ornate glassware. The red wine flows down her throat, warming her. She relishes it, for the first time feeling a little of the weight lift from her heart. Blum looks around the room, at his computer, his files, and a thousand other things lying just as he left them twenty-two days ago when he rode off. Everything here is waiting for him to come back: objects that want to be touched, tools that want to be used. Nothing in the study shows that he is dead, and Blum still hasn't changed that. It is the first time that Blum has been back in this room; she had simply closed the door, almost as if to shut in what was left of him. The air that he breathed, his personal things, his films, the untidiness on which he insisted—his little bit of freedom, he always said. This room was his retreat, the cave into which he shut himself when he was working, or simply when he wanted to get away from the children. His personal preparation room, he used to say, laughing. The place where he sat and thought.

She has dealt with everything else. His clothes, his shoes she has either given or thrown away. She has emptied his drawers. Only his study was still shut up. The mere thought of clearing it out hurt. Now she is sitting here, drinking wine. Not in pain, not oppressed by her grief. She has it under control, she can sit here drinking her wine and waiting. She has been sitting here for over an hour now, surveying the room. She doesn't yet dare pick anything up, open a drawer, remember more than will do her good at this point. She hesitates, she wants to but she can't. She has time, she has the night ahead of her, and the cellar is full of wine. Two hundred bottles. The thought gives her courage. Another cork comes out. Tears are no longer important, not now. She raises her wineglass and drinks to him, to her husband, her happiness. She remembers the little things: his laughter in the bathroom in the morning, his jokes after the fourth glass of wine, the way he pretended to like DIY. He was so clumsy, he hurt himself so often because he didn't pay attention, he really had no clue what he was doing. What a darling he was.

Summoning all her courage, Blum picks up his cell phone. A little world opens up, his engagements, notes, games. Blum leafs through the records of his time, she smiles because he could be so childish and playful. A grown man, a police officer, playing Tetris. His fingers caressing the display. All those text messages he sent her over the years. Their love went back and forth; a kiss would often come from him only half an hour after they had parted, and then she would send one back. All the messages he sent are stored. What she said, what he said. Memories that do her good now. Blum continues to explore, she plunges in, she swims. She and Mark are on their own for almost two hours. But then Dunya arrives.

Blum opens the folder on his cell that contains all his saved conversations. She really just wants to see what's behind the icon;

she doesn't mean to pry. Suddenly, his voice is back again. Mark breathes and speaks. He is back, a little tap on Play and she can hear him. Talking to a woman, a stranger whom Blum doesn't know. At first she doesn't understand what the woman is talking about, what Mark wants to find out. She just hears his voice, hears the sympathy in it as he speaks to the woman cautiously, almost affectionately. Mark wants her to go on talking, he wants her to tell her story. Blum listens. Seconds pass, minutes. Blum sips her wine, she wants to know who this woman is, why he is talking to her, why she is frightened. She hears Dunya, and Mark trying to reassure her.

"Leave me alone. Please. I haven't done anything."

"You don't have to be afraid of me."

"Leave me alone. Don't touch me. Go away, please. Just go away."

"I want to help you."

"I haven't done anything."

"I know that. I'm not here to take you anywhere. I told you, I only want to talk to you about what happened."

"Go away and leave me in peace. Please."

"I believe you. I believe what you said."

"I was talking nonsense. It was nothing. I was drunk."

"You were under the influence of medicinal drugs. Strong tranquilizers."

"Exactly. I was hallucinating. I made it all up."

"No, you didn't."

"I did. So now go back to your cozy little world. You don't want to stay around here. No one does."

"I can help you to find those men."

"No."

"Trust me."

"I said no."

"Why not?"

"Because you're a man."

"I'm a police officer."

"I've been to the police already. I told you all about it, I begged and pleaded, and you ignored me. You put me in a hospital bed and shook your heads over me."

"I'm sorry that happened. Honestly. I know we ought to have taken it all far more seriously. We shouldn't have doubted your story for a second."

"You should have helped me then, but it's too late now. I'm fine here."

"Living under a highway bridge? You don't even have a roof over your head. Someone has to look after you."

"Who? You? Can I come and live with you? Will you get me a residence visa? Do you really want to look after me? If so then leave me in peace, that's the only way you can genuinely help me."

"It will be all right."

"It won't be all right until those men are dead."

"Please, let's talk about it."

"If I talk to you I'll die. You'll stir up a hornets' nest, and the wasps will get angry. You don't know what that means, but I know they will find me and silence me."

"It won't come to that."

"Not so long as I stay here. No one will look for me here. My life is good now, a thousand times better than it was. I want to forget all that, don't you understand? All of it."

"You mustn't do that. You must remember every detail, and you must tell me all about it. Then I'll find those men and make sure they're taken to court and put behind bars, punished for what they did to you. I promise that nothing will happen to you."

"Why are you doing this?"

"Because I want to help you."

"You should have done that earlier."

"I had the whole city searched after you disappeared from the hospital."

"I was sober when you talked to me the second time."

"You weren't giving me anything to go on. You just stared at the wall. What were we to do? In cases like this we're bound to proceed in a certain way. There was nothing we could do but wait for you to be discharged from the hospital."

"It was a psychiatric hospital. You kept me there, I couldn't get away. It was a secure ward. That doctor spent two weeks trying to persuade me that it didn't happen. He wanted to hear me say I was making it up. So in the end I said okay, he was right, and I left. I took the first opportunity to disappear. I'm only a drug-addicted illegal trying not to be thrown out of your country, that's all."

"No, there's much more to it than that. I'll listen until you've finished your story."

"You wanted to be rid of your little problem as quickly as possible."

"I asked you about it in the hospital, and you could have talked to me then, but you kept quiet."

"Sometimes it's best to keep quiet."

"Listen, I want those men arrested. I am absolutely convinced that you are telling the truth."

"Why?"

"I've seen it in your eyes."

"Seen what?"

"Fear and horror. That was genuine."

"Just go away."

"Tell me your name."

"I don't know my name, or my age. That's the only way I can stay. That's what they told us when they smuggled us in."

"My name is Mark."

"I don't want to know."

"I have a wife and two children. I live in Elisabethstrasse, and I'm going to stay here until you talk to me."

"Mark, then?"

"That's right."

"Switch that thing off, Mark."

"It's only for me. No one else will hear it."

Through the handset, Blum hears his voice and the voice of Dunya. A homeless woman telling her story. Mark telling her about his private life to make her trust him. Hesitantly, Dunya began to remember, opening up more and more. He didn't talk to Blum about her, didn't tell her anything, not a word, although the case was clearly occupying his mind. Mark was trying to put a mistake right, talking to her in his own time. There are over twenty files on his phone, always with her voice. Twenty conversations with a woman whose experiences are unimaginable. Conversations that Blum should never have heard, detailed records of a crime, recorded around the city: under the highway, in his car, in underground parking garages, in secret, hidden places. Dunya was afraid, terribly afraid, and Mark took her fear seriously.

Blum checks the dates; she wants to know if there is more, she wants to know it all now, at once. They met over a period of two weeks. Their last meeting was on the day before the accident. Sometimes Dunya broke off the conversation because her memories hurt her, because she was afraid it would all happen again. The horror: the five men down in the cellar, the groans, the pain, the screaming. As the story of the crime comes over the little loudspeaker Blum knows she is listening to something extraordinary. She sits in Mark's study for hours on end, listening to those two voices. Again and again she wants to stop the recording and delete those files. She doesn't want to hear his voice comforting Dunya; she doesn't want to hear her weeping in his arms during their fourth conversation. She would rather not imagine it. Wordless minutes, the closeness that she can sense between them. His closeness to another woman. Blum sits alone at his desk. Never mind what Dunya went through, never mind if it was purely pity on his part, Blum doesn't want to know. Dunya was in his arms, and Mark was drying her tears.

Dunya. Blum thinks of her as she finishes her wine, gulping the last of it down. Why did she suddenly have to intrude, why couldn't Blum just be content with the wine and Mark's desk, why did she have to be curious? Why couldn't she just return the phone to its default settings and sell it on the Internet? Without wondering what it could tell her? Why now? Why does she now have to think of something so awful it is beyond belief? Why is his voice so beautiful? Why can't she stop listening?

All night long she listens to Dunya and Mark. Until the sun rises, the wheel of time turns again and wrenches her out of his life. Until, dazed, she opens his study door and lies down in her bed. She waits until the children come and get into bed with her, snuggling up against her. They crawl under the covers, as they do every morning, and she takes time to soothe them, as she does every morning too. She loves Uma and Nela, but her heart is pounding in her chest.

9

A Ducati Monster 900. The motorcycle Mark doted on, his second great love after Blum, a magnificent machine. He could enthuse for hours about the purring of the engine, an incomparable sound, music to his ears. Mark had loved to ride fast, even where it was forbidden, speeding along the highway and the country roads. Never mind how much Blum worried, he had to do it. He wanted to feel the slipstream of air as the road passed by. *I can't help it. I'll be back, darling, don't worry. It's not that bad, you're exaggerating, my flower.* He found it hard to explain just what it was that fascinated him so much about his Monster 900, his baby. A beauty of a motorcycle. Two chatty men are now unloading it from the trailer.

It gleams in the sun, exactly as it was before. In fact it's new, courtesy of the insurance company. Two weeks ago, Massimo asked her what she wanted to do: did she want the money or a replacement? Blum simply said yes, lost in thought, and asked Massimo to fix everything. Then, after a while, the phone call came saying it was about to be delivered. And here is his motorcycle now. As if it were his voice. It is standing outside the villa, she almost thinks that Mark will come through the door and out into the garden any minute now and mount it. Almost. Blum gives the men a tip and sits down on the bench. You can see everything from the bench, the children, the gate leading from the garden out into the street, the motorcycle. Blum just sits there, thinking about what happened last night. About Mark, and about Dunya, and what seems to have happened to her. What Dunya said, what she had experienced, what Mark believed. He saw it in her eyes. Even if the psychiatrist diagnosed her as delusional. But Mark saw it in her eyes.

It's quiet on the bench. She wants to be taken in comforting arms, she would like to be back in his study, she would like to understand what happened. She wants to listen to it all again sober. It's like a dream that she can only vaguely remember, a nightmare that she has rejected, pushing it out of her life. Blum doesn't want to believe that the woman was telling the truth, she wants Mark to have been wrong, she wants confirmation that Dunya really was delusional. So it was nothing more than the fantasies of a drug addict. None of it is true. It mustn't be true. Because her life can't get worse than it already is. Because the sun is shining. Because the children are playing on the swing. Because this is the first time for weeks that Karl has come into the garden.

Karl has hardly said a word since Mark died. He withdrew to the second floor, sat in his armchair for days, shedding tears. Even the children couldn't comfort him. He asked to be left in peace, said he wanted to be alone. It was only at Reza's insistence that Karl opened his door and let them fill his fridge. Karl has lost his son. Karl tries to smile. Karl sits down beside her on the bench.

"How are you doing, Blum?"
"It still hurts all the time."
"Yes."
"It's good to see you here with us."

"How about the children?"

"They'll live."

"And the motorcycle?"

"It's back—over there."

"Why?"

"Mark loved it."

"So he did."

"I'm going to ride it."

"Are you?"

"Yes."

"But you're afraid of it."

"Yes."

"But you still want to ride it?"

"Fear is crippling."

"I was always afraid for him."

"He did as he wanted."

"He was a good boy."

"He was more than that, Karl."

"We'll get through this, Blum."

"Yes, we will."

They sit in silence. Karl takes Blum's hand and holds it firmly. Nothing exists but their hands, the children, and the motorcycle. A summer's day in the garden. They have said all they need to say, Karl and Blum. There is understanding and affection between them. Blum likes him; she has never regretted asking Karl to come and live with them. He is like a benevolent household spirit. A household spirit resuming his duties. Karl is back, he won't creep away again; he says he has missed the children and wants to go on living, even if it hurts. Wants to go on living, like Blum, go on pushing the swing back and forth.

Blum doesn't wear a helmet. She puts the key in the ignition and presses the button. The Monster purrs. She waves to the children and accelerates out through the gateway and into the road, without glancing at the way the Rover came from. She accelerates. Blum with the wind in her face, with flies in her face. She simply turns the handlebars and feels what happens. How fast she is going. Down the road of houses and onto the highway, eyes narrowed, seeing only a slice of the world flying past. She shifts gears, twists the throttle, increases her speed. Never mind what happens, never mind where she is going. There's only Blum and the road.

She hasn't ridden a motorcycle since she passed her test. A girl she knew at school died in a crash soon after taking the test herself. Dead, just like that, exactly how Mark died. That fear has accompanied her until now. Whenever Mark wanted her to ride with him she said no; she was afraid of dying. But now she is tearing down the highway without leathers, without a helmet, with nothing to protect her except her exuberance, her thoughtlessness, her closeness to death itself, her longing to be with him. She is riding at 190 kilometers per hour, with tiny creatures sticking to her skin, her face pricked by needles. Ride on faster, 220 kilometers per hour. Overtake, hear the sound of the engine, go on and on. Breathe. Die.

10

Blum wanted to understand him. Why he liked and needed that sense of speed. She wondered why he was prepared to die. Every time he accelerated, every time he broke the speed limit, he must have felt he was flying. But he had a family, children, love. A moment would have been enough, a brief moment of inattention. *I love it*, he said. *It's like a song, like dancing, like champagne. You must try it, Blum, just once. I'll look after you.* He'd been trying to persuade her for years to get on the bike and share that sensation with him. She'd said no for so long. Now she has felt what he felt. It was like falling, like nothing else mattered, nothing existed but herself.

She has been riding for an hour. No one has stopped her; no police, no speed camera. She has been gambling with her life for an hour, has imagined her head striking the median strip, crashing into the windshield of an oncoming vehicle. She pictured her death as she rode. She died in full color, and came home uninjured. The world is in order. Karl is putting the girls to bed, Reza is unloading a body from the van.

"Thank you, Reza."
"You don't have to say that."
"Yes, I do, Reza. Nothing here would work without you."

"It's all right."

"Who do you have there?"

"A woman from the nursing home. We had to carry her out through the kitchen."

"Why through the kitchen?"

"They didn't want the other inmates to see that someone had died."

"Inmates?"

"Residents."

"Why through the kitchen, for God's sake?"

"Because they didn't want to remind the inmates that their days are numbered too."

"We agreed on *residents*, right?"

"That's fine by me."

"Her family?"

"Coming tomorrow. They want to see her one last time. The grave's booked, the funeral's organized."

"Reza, you're the best. If you need more help, just say so."

"Everything's fine."

"Is it really?"

"Well, no."

"You don't talk about how you're feeling."

"Mark was my friend. It's like a cake without candles."

"A cake?"

"Mark was the candle on the cake."

"I know."

"He was just blown out."

"I know. It's dark without him. But today Karl said that we'll get through this."

"Did he? That's good. Very good."

"We will, Reza. We'll get through it together, you, Karl, the girls, and me."

"Yes."

"It will get better."

"When?"

"Soon, Reza, soon."

Blum goes upstairs. She almost believes it herself; for a moment something positive flares in her, something like hope. Riding the motorcycle was an intoxicating sensation. She has survived, she has felt what he felt, she has challenged her fate. She knows she is meant to live, not die. The decision has come down in favor of life, of the children, of everything that hasn't happened yet. And in favor of Dunya. She is going to find out what happened, find out about that woman and what terrifies her so much. Blum wants to know; something tells her that it is important, that it is not delusion but truth. Mark believed that, so she believes it too. He wanted to help the woman, and so does she. She has no alternative, she has heard what happened to Dunya, and she can't pretend that it didn't. She pressed Play. There's nothing else she can do; she will listen to everything again. She looks in on the children, lies down with them for a little while, kisses them, and disappears into his study.

She sits in his chair, the cell phone in her hand, listening to that incredible story. The abduction of three people, rape, imprisonment, horror for years on end. It had all begun harmlessly enough; they were supposed to start a new life working in the mountains, escaping an impoverished country. She had been smuggled into Austria, and wanted to leave her native Moldavia far behind. There were no prospects for her there, even her degree was no help; there was no work for an interpreter. She had no future; the only thing she could do was speak German. It seemed like a good idea to go to Germany or Austria. The people-smugglers promised her a good life, work in a nice hotel, first as a chambermaid, maybe later at the reception desk. The pay was good, everything seemed perfect, she had gotten into the country with no difficulty, and all their promises had come true. The money she had paid them was a good investment.

Her new home was the Annenhof designer hotel in the ski resort town of Sölden. A hostel for the staff, good food. It didn't bother her that she wasn't insured, wasn't officially in Austria, so the hotelier could save a lot of money. She would have been happy for everything to continue as it was; she had made a new life for herself, had even found new friends among other illegals on the staff. They were busy hands working unseen in the kitchen, the laundry, the rooms; no one set eyes on them, and they were forbidden to go out. The hotelier didn't want any problems, so no contact with the local villagers was the rule, and Dunya kept it. She went for walks first thing in the morning or late in the evening. When everyone else was asleep, she was out and about, breathing the mountain air, and enjoying it. When she had saved enough money she planned to go to a big German city, Hamburg or Berlin. She wanted a residence permit and a proper life, and for a little while she believed that it was possible. That the world was good, there was something outside Moldavia, something better. For a few months she believed that.

She had come to Austria almost exactly five years ago. Mark wanted to know the whole story, from beginning to end. He had won her confidence, and so she talked. Mark didn't want her to overlook a single thing, he wanted to be sure that the story fit; he listened, asking questions now and then. Again and again he soothed her fears, assuring her that nothing would happen to her, that she was safe. He gave her his word. And she told her story, which had begun on a minibus. Nine of them had crouched there, perched under the loading area; they had been on the road for over a day and a half, with nothing to eat or drink. They hadn't seen daylight again until they arrived in the Tyrol. Mark wanted to know the names of the people-smugglers, which of them had made contact with the hotel, who had met them when they arrived, where her eight companions had gone. Mark pressed her, but gently; he didn't want to frighten her off, he went cautiously. He was looking for leads; he had to begin somewhere, and something in what she was saying must help him. But it was all so vague. Dunya didn't know the answers to many of his questions, and there was a good deal that she couldn't remember. What had happened five years ago was so far in the past, and between then and now there was so much suffering, so much pain, she had been given so many narcotics. Nothing she said led to people Mark could question, however hard he tried, Dunya couldn't help him, not in the way he would have liked. She sat beside him in the car as he tried to find out more.

"Please, Dunya. You must remember."

"I really did think I'd gotten lucky at last. My parents practically starved so that I could study at college. They wanted my life to be better than theirs."

"Your life isn't over yet."

"No, it's over. Nothing can happen now to make up for—"

"Are your parents still alive?"

"I don't know. I was going to bring them here later. I really believed that would happen. I promised them it would."

"We'll find those men, Dunya. They will be punished for what they did, and you'll get your life back, I'll make sure of that. You'll see your parents."

"You shouldn't be giving me false hope."

"It can only get better now, Dunya, but you must tell me

everything—everything, you understand? Every tiny detail, every-thing that seemed strange about the hotel. Tell me about the evening before it began. Until I have something concrete to go on I can't investigate officially. I'm doing this off the books. Officially you don't exist. So come on, Dunya, give me something, anything."

"Ilena and I played cards that evening. It was all the same as usual. We'd finished work, the staff hostel was lovely. We even had a little pool there. It mattered to the hotelier that we were happy, he said."

"What was he like?"

"Nice."

"Johannes Schönborn?"

"Yes."

"He's in politics these days. The hotel doesn't belong to him anymore. He sold it four years ago."

"Then why are we driving there now?"

"To help you remember."

"There's nothing, however often you ask me. I went to sleep, and when I woke up I was in that cellar. I went to sleep in the hostel and I wasn't there when I woke up. It was the same for Ilena and Youn."

"The other two."

"Yes. Ilena was in the minibus with me."

"In the minibus taking you out of Moldavia?"

"That's right."

"Where is she now?"

"She's dead."

"Dead?"

"She bled to death."

"Why? What happened?"

"She had a baby. We were on our own—Youn and I tried to help her, but the blood wouldn't stop."

"In the cellar."

"She died in my arms. Youn was holding the baby."

"Dunya?"

"Yes?"

"Is that the truth?"

"Yes."

"Please, you must tell me whether this is really true."

"How often do I have to say it?"

"You are telling me that your friend had a baby and died in your arms. In a cellar somewhere, a cellar where you were all locked up."

"Yes, that's right."

"I believe you. But you know how it sounds . . ."

"Why would I make it up? Tell me why."

"What happened to the baby?"

"They took it away."

"Where?"

"How would I know?"

"What about Ilena?"

"They shouted and swore, they were beside themselves. They didn't like having blood all over the place. Or for her to have died just like that. The huntsman gave us something to knock us out, and then it went dark. I don't know what happened to her."

"The huntsman?"

"How many more times? I've told you and all the other officers before you."

"I know, I've read the records, but I'd like to hear it from you. Just once more, please. This is important, Dunya."

"He was the one who shot us with the tranquilizing darts. He hunted us down, we ran round the cellar and he shot at us. Like animals. He found it fun."

"What about Youn?"

"I don't know. He was still in the cellar. He's probably dead as well. I don't know."

"Why didn't he go with you?"

"He hadn't come round yet. I shook him, I tried to drag him away with me, but he was too heavy. I couldn't wait. I had to get out of there, the door was open, don't you understand? I wanted him to come with me. I really did try everything. They hadn't locked the door, it was open, and I had to go—had to run for it."

"What did you see?"

"Nothing."

"What did you see when you reached the road? Did anyone meet you? Can you remember any building? Did anyone speak to you, did you call for help? What did you do? Please, you must remember."

"I just ran."

"Where to?"

"A long way away."

"There must have been something there. A place name on a sign, a mountain with a particular shape, a shop, a factory, something that you can remember?"

"I told you, I just ran. I wanted to get away. I don't know what was there or where I was. And then I was in that truck."

"Had you been trying to stop cars?"

"I don't know."

"Where was it, Dunya? Where? We have to find Youn. You must remember something that will tell me where that damn cellar is."

"I don't."

"Were there a lot of people around? Was it somewhere in the countryside?"

"There was only that stinking truck driver."

"He wanted to help you?"

"No, he said he just wanted a bit of fun. I remember that."

"Couldn't he see that you needed help?"

"I don't know."

"He must have noticed there was something the matter with you."

"Yes, that's why he threw me out of his cab."

"What did he look like?"

"I don't know."

"What kind of truck was it?"

"No idea."

"Please, Dunya, give me something."

"There's nothing to give. He was just a sleazy man making jokes. I was dazed, I wasn't right in the head yet, I kept tipping over. All I remember is the road, and the way he laughed. I'd gotten away after five years. Five years, do you understand? And then there was a hand on me again, on my thigh. I screamed and I didn't stop until he opened the door and threw me out, just like that."

"At the service station where my colleagues found you?"

"I don't know."

"Well, they brought you in from there."

"Yes, maybe."

"I really want to know where to look for that cellar, Dunya."

"It was such a lovely feeling."

"What was?"

"Being alone at last, just lying there. On the tarmac in some shitty parking lot. I was free again and none of them were there. Not a single one of them. Only me, do you understand? There was only me."

11

Uma doesn't want to eat. Nela makes a mess of the kitchen floor, spills water over it, throws her pasta across the room. It's midday. Blum watches them. Blum leaves them alone. She knows two things. First, she must look after the children, love them, give them all the things she never had herself. Second, she must find Dunya. The woman talking on the cell phone, the woman whom Mark met so often right before his death. Blum wants to look into her eyes, she wants to see if Mark was right.

He must have picked her up, probably at the tearoom, she had got food there. They drove to the hotel and went on talking. Mark wasn't letting go, but he had nothing to go on. No lead as to how the men managed to abduct them from their beds. Dunya had no idea. Anyone determined could have walked into the staff hostel; indeed, any tourist could have got access to their bedrooms. The front door was never locked, they had no reason to live in fear. That was why it sounded so incredible, so unlikely that someone had drugged them and taken them out of the house. Three grown adults abducted from a hotel, just like that, unnoticed. In Sölden, a famous center of winter tourism, with crowds milling on the slopes, in the boutiques, and in the après-ski bars, with Tyrolean charm for sale, wood-paneled rooms where caviar and champagne are served. Blum knows what the place is like; she and Mark had been skiing there, they had drunk tequila and danced to meaningless songs. Sölden is like any other Tyrolean resort. Anyone would doubt the feasibility of abducting people from it. But Mark didn't. And Blum doesn't either.

Why is she getting involved in his work, why is she interested in it? She can't help herself. She has to follow it up, she can't just sit there pretending nothing has happened. There is a terrified woman out there. A woman who was abducted and locked up for five years, raped and abused. What Blum has heard doesn't allow her to doubt for a minute that she must find out whether it is true. Whether Mark was on the trail of some major and dreadful crime. *Why would I make up a story like that?* Dunya asked. Blum wants to know. And she wants Uma to finally finish her pasta, she wants Nela to stop rubbing tomato sauce into her face.

Ilena, Youn, Dunya. And five men who kept coming back to have their fun. To hurt their captives, to cause relentless pain. As she watches her daughters, innocent and smiling, she wants to banish the thought from her mind. She doesn't want to spend a second longer thinking about those recorded conversations, Mark's questions, Dunya's answers. Yet the story won't go away and she can't think of anything else. From Sölden to the service station near the Italian border. None of what happened will go away, it will stay in her mind all day and all night.

12

Blum no longer feels the pain that has been eating away at her for three whole weeks; she has almost suppressed her longing for him. That feeling has gone, leaving only Dunya. And Mark. Somehow it is as if he has come back to life and she is sharing something with him, she has discovered something he kept hidden. Mark, her husband, her love, the father of her children. He lives on in the conversations that she listens to as she drives through the city searching for Dunya—a stranger to her, a woman without a face. All that Blum knows of her is her voice and that she comes from Moldavia. Blum knows that she speaks extraordinarily good German and is homeless, living somewhere under the highway. This woman without a surname who has suddenly changed everything.

She doesn't say a word to anyone. She has decided to keep quiet for the moment; first she wants to talk to Dunya herself. Only then will she go to Karl or Massimo and ask for help. If it's true. If she can find Dunya. Innsbruck is not a large city, but it is difficult to find someone who doesn't want to be found. Blum prepares for a long search; the staff at the soup kitchen can't give her any information. No one knows a woman called Dunya, the name means nothing to the homeless people Blum speaks to. Even money can't persuade them to tell her where to look. Dunya has left no trace. All Blum can do is search the city, the parks, under the bridges, under the highway. She drives around for hours, walks for hours, but to no avail. There is no Moldavian woman speaking almost unaccented German, no sign of her for three days.

Then, suddenly, there she is, in the supermarket. A slender woman in old clothes. She looks too beautiful, too radiant to be homeless. Dunya is carrying a bag of bottles; she wants to exchange them for money, but the machine isn't working. The salesgirl comes and takes the bottles from her, sorts them into crates and writes out a voucher for the cash. Nothing has changed yet, Blum is still searching, she is on the point of giving up, she has searched every nook and cranny of this town, has checked every place where someone might hide. But Dunya wasn't there. Dunya had disappeared. Now they are standing side by side.

Dunya takes the voucher from the salesgirl. Blum puts the rice noodles that she has taken off the shelf into her shopping cart and continues up the aisle. She doesn't see Dunya shaking her head and opening her mouth, she only hears her asking the salesgirl to check her figures again. *The sum is fifty cents short*, she says. The salesgirl is impatient, she doesn't want to check her sums, she is sure she got them right. But the familiar voice goes on claiming those fifty cents. Blum turns around. *There's no need to kick up such a fuss for fifty cents*, says the salesgirl. But Dunya insists. Politely, but loud and clear, she demands her fifty cents and makes the salesgirl alter the figure on the voucher. It is the voice that Blum has been trying to track down for the past three days.

Blum looks at Dunya. She has imagined her differently, wounded, more damaged. From all she has heard, this woman must be devastated, there ought to be nothing left of her, not an attractive feature on her face, not a spark of hope. But her expression betrays none of what has happened to her. Briefly, Blum wonders whether the voice is really hers, but only briefly. Then she is sure, she knows it beyond any shadow of doubt. She follows her through the supermarket, making purposefully for the cash desk, where Dunya gives the cashier her voucher, takes her money, and leaves, with Blum in pursuit. Blum has abandoned her shopping cart; she mustn't lose Dunya, she must follow her, speak to her.

Dunya crosses the parking lot quickly and reaches the bank of the River Inn. She walks along the riverside promenade, with Blum on her heels. They couldn't be in a better place, there is almost no one else around. Blum takes a moment to get her breath back and formulate a plan. It's happening so fast. A few moments ago, Blum had been on the point of giving up, but now she has found her quarry. She will approach Dunya when they reach the pedestrian bridge. She has until then to suppress the images flooding her mind. Suddenly she feels envy. She feels it everywhere, her heart is crying out again, the pain is back. Everything hurts. Maybe Mark had fallen in love with her. She imagines Mark and Dunya walking side by side along this promenade, sitting on a bench together, talking. Dunya pouring out her heart to him, confiding everything, showing him her innermost being. In her mind's eye, Blum sees her naked before him. Sees him embracing this beautiful foreign woman. With every step she takes, the scenario becomes more real. Blum doesn't want to talk to the woman anymore, Blum wants her to disappear. Go away. Walk on. Blum stops, and closes her eyes.

Why didn't she just give the phone away? Why did she insist on listening to it all? Why does this woman have to be so beautiful?

Why can't she just talk to her and ignore the noise in her head? Why is she afraid Mark was unfaithful? Suppose he had touched Dunya? Kissed her, caressed her in her despair. Suppose Dunya had simply said yes, had accepted his understanding, his kindness, his instinctive urge to rescue. Like Blum had eight years before. Terrible things had happened to Dunya, but there was more than pity in his voice. Much more. Blum is afraid of opening her eyes, afraid of following, afraid of finding out. She does it all the same. She opens her eyes and she runs. *Dunya!*

"Please stop. Dunya, please. I only want to talk to you."

"Why? What do you want? How do you know my name?"

"From Mark."

"Get lost."

"I'm his wife."

"You'd better get lost."

"Wait! Talk to me, just for a minute. Please."

"I've talked enough."

"I know."

"You don't know anything."

"I know all about it. I've heard the recordings."

"That bastard."

"What do you mean?"

"Did the two of you enjoy it? Listening in on me? Did you sit back and eat popcorn? Was it a good show?"

"No."

"He told me no one would ever hear what I said."

"He never played it to anyone."

"But you're here, right?"

"I was going to delete everything on his cell. And then I stumbled on his conversations with you."

"Go away. Don't ever come near me again."

"I'm Blum."

"And I'm Dunya, now get fucking lost."

"Mark took everything you said very seriously."

"I don't want you to know my story."

"It's too late for that now."

"I want you to get the hell away from me."

"He believed you. And he liked you."

"Well, that didn't do me any good. First he squeezes the story out of me, then he leaves me high and dry. He's no different from the others."

"No, he was different."

"Then why hasn't he come back?"

"He really would have come back, you can believe me."

"He told me he'd take care of everything. He said he'd help me. So why didn't he? Go on, tell me. Why not?"

"Because he's dead."

"What? What did you say?"

"He died four weeks ago—"

"How?"

"In an accident."

"Please, no."

"I think of it every minute of every day. But he's dead and he won't be coming back. We're on our own. Do you understand?"

"How did it happen? How did he die?"

"He was run over."

"What happened to the driver?"

"It was a hit-and-run. The driver hasn't been traced. He disappeared."

"Oh no. Please no."

"Mark died instantly."

"You'd better stay away from me."

"Why?"

"I really did think it would be all right. Believe me, I didn't want that to happen."

"Didn't want what to happen?"

"Didn't want him to die."

"It was an accident."

"That was no accident."

13

They sit at the kitchen table. Blum has cooked for Reza, Karl, the children, and Dunya. She brought the woman home with her, led her back to the parking lot, and got her into her car. Blum ignored Dunya's protests and dismissed her objections; she wasn't going to let the woman out of her sight. Blum wanted to know what Dunya meant when she said it was no accident. She shouted at Dunya, begging her to tell her what she knew. But Dunya merely shook her head, apologizing over and over again. She tried to escape, but Blum restrained her. Wordlessly, anxiously, they sat in the car as Blum drove to the villa. Dunya didn't want anyone else to get hurt. *I'm so sorry*, she said.

Dunya seemed surprised to find that the villa and garden belonged to an undertaker's business. Hesitantly, she shook hands with Reza and Karl, and did not move from Blum's side. She was shaken, overwhelmed by so much hospitality, by the fact these people she didn't know were smiling at her. As Karl opened the wine he didn't hear Dunya asking in a whisper why Blum had done it, why she had brought her home, why she hadn't simply looked away like all the others.

Blum was burning inside, but she tried to smile and said nothing. All she wanted was the truth. She wanted to know exactly what had happened to Mark, and she wanted to persuade Dunya to stay. In silence, she tipped spaghetti into boiling water. Dunya couldn't hear any of what was going on inside Blum. Doubt, fury, hatred. Soundlessly, Blum was screaming for the truth. *If you're lying, then stop. If you're telling the truth then get out, leave us in peace, don't put us in harm's way. I wish you'd just say something, Dunya. Say something? I want to see what's there. After that I'll throw you back into the sea, I just want to know if what you say can be true. Or if you're out of your mind. Because surely it can't be true. No one would ever do such things to you. Dunya, tell me you were just using Mark because you were lonely, because you needed someone to listen to you and take you in his arms. Tell me that. Anything else is madness. No human being could endure it. Tell me it isn't all true. Please.*

Blum was staring at Dunya with a forced smile. She wore that smile while the pasta cooked, minutes passing without words, only the meeting of glances and the chopping of onions. She wanted to weep, scream, fly off the handle; she wanted to switch everything off—Dunya, this day, life. Simply turn off a switch as she was dicing the tomatoes. But for the moment she needed to act as if everything were all right, as if none of it had happened. Smile, lift the corners of your mouth, and press your lips together. How she was burning, how her ideas were tumbling over one another. Because the mere idea of what the woman had been through was so inhuman.

And now they sit eating the pasta and it feels almost as though Dunya has always been there, at the large kitchen table. They don't talk about Mark, although there is nothing Blum would have liked more, nor do they talk about the undertaker's business. There is no talk of their dead. They just talk about the weather, the approaching autumn, about the backyard that Karl and Reza will be preparing for winter. And about the children. Uma and Nela are curious, and want to know more about this stranger in their home. They have shown her everything, and willingly let her have their bedroom. Taking her hands in theirs, they have shown Dunya round the house; she is their mother's new friend and an old acquaintance of their father. It doesn't seem to bother them, or anyone else round the table, that she says so little. They eat and drink, an extended family at the dining table with spaghetti, salad, and wine. Plenty of wine. After Blum has put the little rascals to bed, they open another bottle, and it is almost an enjoyable evening, the first time since Mark's death that they have all come together. Wine washes the darkness away for a little while, and Karl even tells jokes. Then his eyes begin to close, and he falls asleep in his chair. Reza says good night and takes the old man upstairs.

Blum and Dunya are at the kitchen table, their glasses freshly filled. In another life this is where the day would be ending. But for these two it goes on, for hours if required. Blum has so many questions. Everything that Dunya said this afternoon fills the room. Now that they are alone again Blum is afraid of what Dunya was suggesting. That Mark's death wasn't an accident, but murder.

At the kitchen table, in the middle of the night, Dunya says so again. She believes that someone was lying in wait for Mark. Waiting for him to come out of the gates. One of those five men stepped on the accelerator and drove straight into Mark. Dunya knows it, senses it, does not believe in coincidences. *It was murder*, she says. Blum contemplates the possibility. There is so much which is hidden.

"Please, Dunya. How can you be so sure?"
"Because I know those men. They'd do anything to avoid being

caught. They'd spend the rest of their lives in prison for what they did."

"You're talking about murder."

"Yes."

"Mark never harmed anyone."

"He stirred up a hornets' nest. The last time we met, he told me that he might have found one of the men. The photographer."

"What did he find?"

"I don't know. He just said I wasn't to worry."

"Nonsense, that wasn't on the tape. It can't be true."

"He'd already switched off his phone, he didn't want anyone to hear. No one, you understand. It was the last thing he said to me. Then he left. And didn't come back. I hated him for that."

"But they wore masks, didn't they? All the time? You said you never saw their faces all those years."

"No, only the masks."

"Then how could he have found the man? How, tell me?"

"I don't know."

"There are hundreds of photographers in the Tyrol. And no one says he has to come from the Tyrol anyway. No one knows where that cellar is. You could have been in Bavaria, or in Italy. You were found just by the Italian border."

"I'm so sorry. I can only tell you what I told him myself."

"Now you must tell me everything, one last time."

"I can't go through it all again."

"Please. Do it for Mark."

"My story killed him. And it will kill you too."

14

Blum twists the throttle again. She is wearing a helmet, she has bought herself leathers. She keeps reminding herself that she has children, that she doesn't want to die. Hence the helmet, hence the leathers. But still she rides fast. Along the highway, over the bridge into the Ötz Valley. There are many bends in the road, but it's only twenty minutes before she reaches the village where she may find answers. Everything that Dunya has told her began there. In the staff hostel five years ago. Someone must know something, someone must have noticed that Dunya was missing.

Blum is riding twice as fast as she should. She races through Ötz, a little Tyrolean village. Ignoring the disapproving looks of people by the road, she swiftly leaves the village behind her, she must go on, she must get to Sölden quickly. Mark found something, Blum knows it. She now knows that Dunya is right and there can be no doubt about that, none at all. She speeds past roadside shrines as the road winds upwards. Everything that has happened lies ahead of her. Blum spent almost all night trying to soothe Dunya's fears, stroking her hair and listening to her story. Dunya told her things she hadn't told Mark, terrible things that made her weep, that brought her to seek protection in Blum's arms. An evil fairy tale in which Dunya plays the starring role. A horror film about five men, including this photographer.

Five men. The photographer, the priest, the huntsman, the cook, and the clown. Dunya has described each of them. She tried to remember everything they did, she wanted to help Blum. She told her all about the pictures the photographer took. How enthusiastic he was, how passionately he spoke of his work. His photographs would make him famous, they were unique. Compositions on the subject of pain. How he talked to the others about his projects, his achievements, taking photos like a man possessed. Youn's face while the priest smashed into him from behind. Youn's screams, his gaping mouth, his desperation. And Ilena, her eyes vacant because nothing could hurt her anymore. There was only a void, never mind how hard they struck, how often they thrust into her, how often the clown hit her, pummelling her belly. Only those dazed, empty eyes. The photographer enthused about that effect for minutes on end, saying how unique they were, these moments recorded in pictures. How authentic and true to life, how extraordinarily honest. He tied Dunya down to the table and raped her, taking photographs all the time. If she turned her head away he hit her.

"He photographed you while he was doing that to you?"
"Yes."
"Were you naked?"
"He only took pictures of our faces."
"Only your faces?"
"He thought it was art. He thought he'd be very successful with it."
"Only faces?"
"Yes, whether or not we were naked."

"So not pornography?"

"No, only pain."

"What a sick bastard. And the others went along with that? They didn't object?"

"No, they all liked keeping a record of what they did to us."

"How old is this man?"

"Under forty, barely."

"His voice?"

"Gentle. Pleasant. Only his voice, though."

"What else did he say?"

"Thousands of things."

"Such as?"

"That he'd photograph me as I lay dying."

"What did he mean?"

"Exactly what he said."

"He was going to kill you?"

"He said he'd fuck me up the ass till I died. Then he was going to take a photo of my lips. He thought my lips were very beautiful. He wanted to take pictures of them when I was dead. After he'd fucked me to death, when my lips weren't touching any longer."

"You're safe here, Dunya."

"There's nothing left of me."

"I'm so sorry about it all. But I'm so glad that you got away, that you're here."

"It's because of me that you're on your own now."

"They killed him, you didn't."

"Do you believe me now?"

"Yes. I'll look after you, Dunya."

Blum took Dunya in her arms. No one in the world needed her more than Dunya; no one was more helpless, more wounded, had more tears. Suddenly there was no room left for Blum's own grief, only this woman, ragged and wounded. Dunya was trembling all over, fear dripped from every word she said. Blum held her firmly. Dunya whimpered. Then, still trembling, she fell asleep.

Blum is on the motorcycle; she has to find the photographer. He is one of the five men who are guilty of Mark's death. And he is the key that will open the door to the truth. Mark had started a stone rolling and the stone had rolled over him. It was no coincidence, Dunya said. The Rover was no coincidence. Mark had to die, he had tracked down the man with the camera, the man who had pressed the shutter thousands of times. This man had recorded the horror for five years, recorded their despair in print, and that was evidence. Evidence that Dunya didn't have. The horror urges Blum on. Never mind how fast she rides, she can't escape it.

Along the mountain road at 160 kilometers per hour. She feels no fear, only rage. No fear of death, no fear of those men, only hatred and the road beneath her, the tires and all that lies ahead. What lies behind her is Mark, and everything they did to Dunya. Blum will find them. Blum will find out who was driving that Rover. She won't stop asking questions, she will dig her teeth into her quarry and refuse to let go.

Blum rides into Sölden. The hotels are closed for the summer. Where crowds will be thronging the sidewalks in winter, all is quiet now. Like many other resorts in the Tyrol, this village only comes alive in the ski season. However hard they try to attract summer tourists, the streets stay empty. Many hoteliers would rather close than cook for a handful of people. Sölden is a mecca for skiing, and for some years now a destination for rich Russians. But there's no trace of them today, no golden ski suits, no three-figure tips, no après-ski bars with music and people getting drunk. Only grass on the slopes, only empty eyesores as far as the eye can see, hiding the mountains. Closed bars, signs pointing to hotels with names suggesting mountain views and Alpine flowers: the Alpenblick, Edelweiss, Bergblick, Alpenrose, Felseneck, Zirbenhof, Lerchen-hof, Rosenhof. And then the Annenhof, behind the parking lot for the ski lift. How abandoned it all is, how dismal. She tries to imag-ine living here, waiting for winter, living only half a life. The two hikers coming towards Blum look lost but then she sees them go up steps—to the Annenhof, one of the few hotels now open. The hotel where it all began. Blum parks the bike. She goes through the lobby to the bar. First she'll try the waiter. She'll talk to him casually over a beer, maybe flirt with him. Whatever it takes. Blum isn't going to leave this hotel until she knows more. Blum wants gossip, rumor, she wants a look behind the scenes. *That's where you find things out*, Mark always said. She sits down with a smile at the empty bar and orders. She feels almost as though she's alone in the hotel. The waiter is polishing glasses; there's nothing for him to do but talk to Blum about the past.

"A beer, please."
"A large one?"
"Absolutely."
"Come far, have you?"
"Just a little round-trip."
"Pretty, isn't it?"
"You think so?"
"Don't you?"
"No."
"What are you doing here, then?"
"What are *you* doing here? You sound as if you come from the east of Germany. That's not exactly round the corner."
"There's work here. And I get to serve pretty ladies like you."

"Why, thank you."

"You're welcome. And by the way, the beer's from there too."

"Why's that?"

"The boss is from the east."

"In the olden days the Germans were guests here."

"They still are."

"Ah, but now they get served by Germans."

"So?"

"Don't get me wrong, I'm glad you have work and I'm glad you're here. I'm just surprised there aren't any Tyroleans wanting the jobs these days."

"It was the same before."

"Was it now?"

"Eastern Europeans used to work here. There weren't many Tyroleans around the place, even before."

"Eastern Europeans?"

"That's right."

"Working legally?"

"No."

"Illegals?"

"Among other things, that's why this place was closed down."

"Is that right?"

"No idea. I mean, what does a guy from the east of Germany know? I wasn't even here at the time."

"I like guys from the east of Germany."

"Hey, you're pretty funny."

"Am I?"

"And you look damn good."

"And you're chatting up a guest."

"What else is there for me to do?"

"How long have you been here, then?"

"Three years."

"Then you didn't work for the old boss?"

"No, none of us here now did. They changed the whole staff. I suppose they wanted a fresh start."

"That's a pity. I need to talk to someone who worked here five years ago."

"Why?"

"I was in love with a waiter at the time. Only I didn't realize it until too late, and now I don't know where to find him."

"Very romantic."

"Yes, isn't it? I wonder if you can help me. Who might know him? Did any locals work here? There must be someone who knows the waiters from back then."

"Seems like the hotel was swept clean overnight. Three-quarters of the staff weren't properly registered back then. The old boss didn't take that stuff so seriously."

"I heard he's in local government now."

"So I heard. Sounds like he got out just at the right time. An investor from the east made him an offer, and it was all signed and sealed in no time. I reckon this man Schönborn had so many skeletons in his closet he couldn't stay here. They might even have locked him up. So he bolted."

"That's what they say about him in the village, do they?"

"Exactly."

"And what else?"

"Nothing I'd bet a single cent on, it's probably all nonsense, spread by the former doorman here, who hasn't a good word to say about Schönborn. What's more, the old doorman drinks a fair bit, so no one really believes him. All nonsense, like I said. So I prefer to keep my mouth shut and stick to the facts."

"What was he saying?"

"No idea, you'll have to ask him yourself. But watch out. The man's not quite right in the head. He used to drink here a lot, so

91

I knew what he was like. Always shooting his mouth off, thought Schönborn was responsible for the mess he'd made of his life. If he'd had things his own way he'd have been managing the hotel by now. Had ideas above his station, poor guy."

"I'd like to talk to him."

"Maybe you'd better not. If he ever knew where your boyfriend went, you can bet he'll have forgotten it by now."

"But it's worth a try, don't you think?"

"Not if you're going to leave me here all alone."

"Sorry, darling."

Blum smiles and gets to her feet. She goes out round the back to the staff hostel, where she pictures three people being loaded into a car unseen, in the middle of the night. A robbery of humans in paradise, a plunge from heaven to hell. Blum plans to find out where that hell is. She gets on her motorcycle and rides away.

15

He lives in a room on the first floor. The building is so shabby, she struggles to find the entrance among the trash. She goes up a crumbling flight of outside steps and knocks. There's a light on, he's there, she can hear him, but all the same it is some time before he comes to the door. Blum has nothing to lose; she feels curious, she wants to know what the man has to say. Anything is better than turning round and going home, even this gnarled man and his schnapps, the devilish faces everywhere.

His name is Sebastian Hackspiel. Blum sits opposite him on a decrepit old sofa. She has made her way through the room, forcing down feelings of disgust and sitting where he suggests. *Call me Hackspiel.* He didn't waste much time asking what she wanted, he merely opened the door, and she followed him down the corridor to the back room. In her professional life Blum has seen a great many things, she has been in hundreds of homes to collect bodies, time and again she has entered rooms no one had prepared, time and again she has seen other people's lives plain and unvarnished. But the spectacle of Sebastian Hackspiel's life is in a class of its own. This house, this room, the masks on the walls, the wrinkled little man holding his woodcarver's knife. There are wood shavings everywhere, pots of paint, brushes, knives, wood, cigarette butts. And bottles emptied of beer and schnapps. He asks her, *Like a drink?* Blum smiles and says yes. Without thinking she empties the glass, and watches him pour her another.

"You've come for a devil?"

"No."

"Bad luck, girl, I only carve devils."

"I'd like to talk to you about the Annenhof."

"A good devil is the only right sort. A good mouth, wide open, with a proper tongue and well-carved horns. That's a proper devil, that is."

"I like your artwork."

"It's not artwork, they're devils."

"I like your devils."

"They're good devils. Handcrafted, see what I mean? I pour all my love into them. My heart in every devil."

"I can see that."

"So you want to talk about the Annenhof? Why?"

"Because my husband is dead."

"And that's the fault of the Annenhof?"

"In a way."

"Well, I'm sorry about that. About your husband, I mean. Being dead. What do you want to know, girl?"

"Everything. What happened back before the hotel changed ownership. Work done on the side, illegal immigrants."

"How do you know about that?"

"A woman who used to be on the staff told me."

"Who?"

"Her name is Dunya. A Moldavian."

"Don't know her. There were so many of them, the whole staff hostel was full of foreigners."

"Maybe you would remember her, though. She's pretty. Black

hair, dark eyes, about five foot four. She shared a room with a girl named Ilena. Another Moldavian."

"I never paid attention to the names. I had enough to do looking after the place."

"But you knew they were illegals?"

"Sure."

"And you didn't say anything."

"Schönborn paid us well to keep quiet."

"Us?"

"All of us who knew about it. That was still a lot cheaper than if he'd registered all those illegals as hotel staff. They worked for peanuts, they were glad to be here in our beautiful Tyrol. They were good and kept quiet and lived in the staff hostel."

"You reported Schönborn to the police. Why?"

"Because he dropped me like a hot potato, he sold the place to a German and scampered."

"And you thought he owed you something?"

"I always kept my mouth shut, I did everything for that dickhead. Then he hands me five hundred euros and waves good-bye."

"That wasn't enough?"

"It was a joke. The gall of it! A humiliation. I always had his back. The show wouldn't have gone on without me."

"You were the life and soul of the Annenhof?"

"Correct."

"So you aided and abetted him?"

"So what if I did?"

"Why did you do it?"

"For the money. Look at this place."

"And what about the illegals?"

"They were all well off here, far better off than where they came from. They even had their own pool."

"Hackspiel?"

"What?"

"Give me another schnapps."

"As many as you like, girl."

"I'm not here to judge you."

"I should think not."

"I'm here because I absolutely have to know more about that hotel."

"It'll cost you."

"How much?"

"Two hundred."

"Is what you know worth that?"

"You bet."

"Well then, cheers. And start talking."

"It's delicate."

"You should be able to get over your inhibitions for two hundred euros."

"Right: even if the pigs don't want to hear it, Schönborn was running a brothel in the cellar."

"What?"

"You heard me. A brothel. For fucking prostitutes. I told you it was delicate."

"A brothel?"

"Officially it was massages only."

"But?"

"But it was a high-class whorehouse. Top quality, understand?"

"You went there?"

"I'm afraid not. Beyond my means. But the women were the best. The guests spent a fortune down there."

"Down where?"

"In the wellness rooms."

"Says who?"

"I do."

"And who else?"

"No one wants to say too much, girl. Those who did know won't want to talk about it, understand?"

"Why not?"

"Because they'd been to the whorehouse, and that doesn't go down well with their wives."

"You mean the locals came for massages as well?"

"That's what they called it."

"But you don't know who, of course. And you can't prove that it was prostitution."

"I know what it was. I was the Annenhof's, shall we say, facto-tum for years."

"But you can't give me the name of anyone who could confirm what you say?"

"I don't want to start a war here in the village, missy. But I can tell you one thing, they went at it like rabbits in that cellar for years. And just before they were going to get busted, Schönborn sold the hotel. He could smell a rat, knew his time would be up in a month or two. The deals on the side, the brothel, and God knows what else."

"These are just rumors, though. You'll have to give me some-thing more for two hundred euros."

"You can have another schnapps if you really want. Cheers, girlie."

"I'm looking for a photographer."

"Like I said, there are only devils here. You won't find a photog-rapher in this place."

"A photographer who had something to do with the Annenhof. Does that mean anything to you?"

"Oh, that's easy. I'm happy to help you out there."

"You will?"

"Schönborn's son is a photographer. I'm sure he had a massage

97

or two on his visits home. Arrogant little dickhead. His name is Edwin."

"Schönborn's son is a photographer?"

"That's right. What's the matter with you, girl?"

"Can it really be that simple?"

"I have no idea what you're talking about, but yes, Schönborn junior is a photographer. He has a studio in Innsbruck, quite the little artist he is. All financed by Papa. Junior is a layabout."

"Hackspiel."

"What?"

"You've really earned those two hundred euros."

"Fine. We should have another drink to that."

"Yes, we should."

Blum drinks. She never imagined it could be so simple. To think that her man is the son of the former hotelier, or at least there's a possibility he is. The man who took the photos. One of the five torturers, perhaps Mark's murderer. *He was often at the hotel while Dunya worked there, he came on weekends*, says Hackspiel. *He used to have a good time with his friends, partying in the mountains; he was the boss's son and acted the part.* Hackspiel dislikes him, hasn't a good word to say about him. Edwin Schönborn was a professional daddy's boy, spoiled rotten. Hackspiel tells stories. None of them make Schönborn a murderer, yet Blum feels that she is on the right track. Hackspiel refills their glasses, and tries to persuade Blum to buy a devil mask. Blum just smiles. The alcohol is warming her, she is excited, planning her next steps. She will go to see Edwin Schönborn, find out whether he has anything to do with it. Or whether it is all just coincidence.

Blum keeps drinking. She doesn't think how she is going to get home, she sits on the shabby sofa listening to the devil-carver.

Much of what he says is nonsense, she guesses, but a lot of it must be true. This crazy old man may have brought her, instantly, to where she wants to be. She wants to believe in this, the simplest solution; she suspects that Mark did the same, that he was investigating the most obvious suspect. Edwin Schönborn had the opportunity to abduct Dunya and the others, he knew his way around the hotel, he could have anesthetized her. It would have been possible for him to plan and carry out the abduction without attracting anyone's attention. Edwin Schönborn, son of one of the most influential men in the Tyrol. Blum will go and see him. Tomorrow. As soon as the world stops swimming before her eyes.

Seven large glasses of schnapps later, Blum can't take any more. She can't ride the bike either. She wants to, but Hackspiel won't let her, takes the key away and pushes her back on the sofa. *You're staying here, girl*, he says. Then he calmly goes on carving. Blum makes a brief phone call to Karl, asking him to put the girls to bed and see to Dunya. The bike broke down, she says, a tire burst, she can't start for home until morning. He mustn't worry, and please will he kiss the girls good night for her. Then she just lies there, watching Hackspiel's knife sink into soft pinewood. For an hour she watches a devil emerging from the wood. Blum sees him taking shape, slowly opening his mouth and baring his teeth. A devil comes into the world. Devils have taken Dunya's life away, men in masks, men without a story, men without names. They are everywhere, on the walls, in Blum's head; she is afraid to close her eyes. Everything is spinning, and however hard she tries to keep her eyelids open, she can't. They are too heavy, the devils push them down.

16

Blum parks outside the District Criminal Investigation Office. Since waking up she has thought of nothing else but the fact she needs help; the situation is too much for her. She must talk to Massimo, confide in him. Since she opened her eyes, she has been thinking she must tell him what she knows. She can't and won't be alone with it; she will put the matter in his hands. She wants to withdraw, look after her children, look after Dunya, help her apply for asylum, maybe find her a job.

It was still dark when she opened her eyes. Hackspiel must have fallen off his chair while he was carving. He was lying on the floor with his limbs outstretched, snoring. The rattle of his snores had woken Blum, roused her from her dreams. She was grateful, because the dreams were terrible. Waking up beside Hackspiel had been a relief. She got up quietly, put two hundred euros on Hackspiel's dresser, and went out into the tail end of the night. It was only five in the morning and the streets were empty. Blum had the highway to herself. Her decision became more and more concrete the closer she came to Innsbruck. Looking for the photographer on her own was dangerous; she knew what these men were capable of. Dunya was probably right to assume the worst, believing that they wouldn't hesitate to kill again. Blum wanted to go home to her children, she didn't want to endanger them. She must protect them, and Karl, and Reza, the people who were closest to her. If the story was true she must stop snooping around. She must go to Massimo quickly, she thinks, as she rides at 200 kilometers per hour with a headache through west Tyrol.

She asks for Massimo at reception. Blum knows he is on night duty; she phoned him yesterday just before setting off for Sölden. He asked how she was. She knows that Massimo would do anything for her, drop whatever he was doing, everything. His wife, his life so far. When he looks at her and touches her, Blum knows. And she is glad he is there, with his strong shoulders, when she feels wounded and small. Blum goes upstairs to the second floor; she knows her way around, she has often been here to collect Mark. Sliding down the banisters with Mark, laughing, chasing her down the steps. Blum opens the door of Massimo's office and takes him by surprise. How glad she is to see his radiant expression, to feel his embrace. *You must help me*, she says.

It doesn't take her long to persuade him to go to a café around the corner. He is pleased to see her, he drives away the devils in her mind, the images that Dunya has planted there. He takes her hand, because she is trembling. She lets him, and pushes the hair back from her face with her other hand. She wonders where to begin. What to say to him. Serve him the whole story for breakfast? Her head hurts. She must drink water, tell him all about it, now. She begins, cautiously, in Mark's study, how she was tidying up his things, how she found the recordings, the woman's strange voice. Massimo listens. At first he says nothing, listens intently, lets Blum talk. He doesn't know what she is getting at yet, what is making her so incoherent. Until the moment she mentions Dunya's name he just listens. Then he interrupts her lovingly and soothes her fears. Blum doesn't get round to telling him what's in the recordings on Mark's cell. Or that she found Dunya and has talked to her, that she is in Blum's house waiting for her return. She doesn't get round to saying that she has been to Sölden and suspects the photographer Edwin Schönborn of being one of the men who tortured Dunya. Or that Mark's death may not have been an accident, but murder. She says none of that because Massimo turns everything upside down, brings bright color to what was dark and gloomy. He reassures her, tells her that what the woman said was nonsense, she was an impressive liar but it was just the talk of a mentally ill woman. Massimo tells her it was all lies. He remembers Dunya very well, he says, and the director of the psychiatric hospital diagnosed her as deluded. Dunya was under the influence of drugs, and ran away from the hospital although everyone wanted to help her. Mark, Massimo, and many others.

Blum listens. Her mouth stays shut; she keeps everything she was going to say to herself. She is speechless, just looks at Massimo and hears the things he says. About Mark and about Dunya. Blum's view of the world suddenly looks different again. What she believed, it seems, was nothing but lies. It was only Mark who insisted on believing that the woman was telling the truth. At the time, Massimo advised Mark to drop his investigation and attend to more important things, but Mark wouldn't listen. He was drilling for oil where there wasn't any oil. It was just another attempt to rescue a pretty young woman on a boat. A pretty young woman in a bed in the psychiatric hospital. Dunya.

Blum says nothing. What Dunya told her, what she was convinced of ten minutes earlier, no longer matters. There is only one thought in her head, and it calls out loud. Why did Mark meet Dunya when everyone advised him against it? Why is there that regret on Massimo's face? What does he know? What did Mark do? Blum is afraid everything will fall apart, that Mark will hurt her. She takes Massimo's hand and asks him to tell her the truth, sparing nothing. She wants him to tell her whether Mark was in a relationship with Dunya. But Massimo says nothing, only that Mark was his friend. He is evasive. He won't say whether Mark was unfaithful to her, whether he was risking their life together. He asks Blum to forget the whole thing, dismiss the recordings as the fantasies of a lost soul and think no more of them. He asks her not to doubt Mark, not for a second.

Blum gets up and goes, goes without saying good-bye. Through the door and out into the street; she needs fresh air, she wants to understand what has just happened. She walks on, putting one foot in front of the other, leaving the motorcycle behind. Air. Walk on and on. Mark is tearing her heart apart again, the noise becomes unbearably loud, the hurt throbs. Every memory she has of Mark is threatened by what Massimo has said. And by what he hasn't said. She doesn't want to, but she pictures Mark and Dunya in a hotel room. After the fourth meeting they couldn't help themselves, they were in love. That notion, which was there from the beginning, burrowing through her body like a worm, is back. He isn't here, can't justify himself, can't take her in his arms and tell her to wake up. And stop dreaming.

Blum hasn't shed tears for days, she has felt close to Mark again because she was doing what he had done. She was trying to follow the same trail as him: they had the same end in view, the same instinct. That Dunya was more than a homeless drug addict. That every word she said was the brutal truth. He had believed that and so had Blum. She still does, even if jealousy cripples her and almost takes away her breath. The idea that her memories might be tainted drives Blum down the street. She must calm down, she must think clearly. Stop doubting Mark. Stop doubting Dunya. Everything happened as she said it did. She believes this woman. She believes in Mark. He met her because he wanted to help her and for no other reason. Never mind what Massimo says. Never mind how impossible it all sounds. Never mind if she is the only person in the country convinced that the cellar and those men exist. Blum has seen the truth in Dunya's eyes. She will take a deep breath, go back to her motorcycle and ride it home. She will hug the children and look up that photographer's number. She will find proof of Dunya's story. She will convince Massimo with facts that show the story is more than a web of lies. That Mark felt nothing for the woman, nothing at all, except pity.

17

Dunya spent the whole day in bed. Karl kept looking in on her as she lay nestled in Nela's pink sheets, safe and protected by the fragrance of the little girls. She slept for hours on end, and only when Karl insisted that she must eat something did she leave the children's room. When Blum called to say that she wouldn't be home that night, Dunya was already asleep. Karl says she was almost like a wounded animal taking refuge in a corner. Dunya was friendly, and kept thanking them for their hospitality, but she wanted to be alone. She said as little as she could to Karl and Reza; she always had a smile for the children, but there was nothing more that she could give them. Karl asked Uma and Nela to be considerate of Dunya, telling them that their mother's friend was very tired, and it had been a long time since she had had a good sleep. He couldn't think up a better explanation.

When Blum got home five hours ago, Dunya was still asleep. She lay in bed like a small child, curled up, legs bent. Blum stood beside the bed as she did when Nela was in it. She looked down at Dunya and felt the very last of her doubts disappear. There she lay, broken, helpless, like a torn scrap of paper. It was probably the first time in years that she had slept in a proper bed, a bed where she had nothing to fear, where no one would hurt her. Her face was peaceful; she was clinging firmly to the quilt. Blum closed the door and went upstairs to Karl. He was running through the apartment with the children on his shoulders.

Blum takes her time. She makes owls with the children, sews little fabric bags, stuffs them with paper, and gets the children to stick on eyes, noses, and beaks. Owls. The girls love owls. Goodness knows why, but they run happily round the house holding their little fabric owls. *We're flying, Mama. We're owls, Mama. Hoo hoo, hoo hoo.* At this moment nothing in their faces shows that they miss their father. That they have realized he won't be coming back. They are simply having fun with owls. Because they don't want the forest where the owls are flying to burn down, because they're not strong enough to run for their lives in the fire. So they don't want to talk about it or be reminded of it. Because it hurts so much. The natural way is to ignore the truth as best they can. Not to keep reviving the sorrow, the tears, the longing for Papa. Playing with owls, with stuffed cats and dogs, immersing themselves in picture books and laughter. But sometimes as best they can isn't good enough.

Uma was standing in the road four days ago, shouting, *Papa. You must come home. Please, Papa, come home.* She had gone downstairs on her own, out of the drive, to the place where he died. Her shouting was loud enough to be heard on the top floors of the house. Blum ran down, picked Uma up, held her close. But she couldn't say anything to soothe Uma's pain, they were both helpless. The empty road hurt. There was nothing to be seen now, no blood, no sign of Mark, only Uma's trembling at a reality that scared her.

The owls fly round the living room while Blum looks for Edwin Schönborn on the Internet, while she clicks his home page and rings his number. The owls land in the bathroom while she phones him and agrees on a date. It's very spontaneous. She decides to play a game. She baits her trap with flattery, saying she doesn't want any other photographer, only him, she wants some nude photos, she's heard he's the best in the country, so it has to be him. Blum doesn't want to wait a day longer, she wants to know, at once. She'd like to discuss the photo shoot with him, she says, she has some ideas and, as chance would have it, she happens to be in the city, money is no object. Blum secures an appointment. She should come to his studio in a hour's time, he says, he looks forward to meeting her. She hadn't thought their meeting could be arranged as quickly as that. Blum ends the call and asks Karl to look after the children again. Then she showers, changes, and drives into town.

Her heart is thudding. There's no time to be lost. It's afternoon on Herzog-Friedrich-Strasse, in the Old Town of Innsbruck. A choice piece of real estate; his rent must cost a fortune. Blum stands at his door and rings the bell. Slowly, she walks upstairs. Blum is breathing deeply, in then out. She must keep her nerve, stay calm. She will meet him without preconceptions, she will just talk to him about photographs, about nudes, about his work. And she will record the conversation, she will take his voice home and play it to Dunya. Blum presses Record, then the studio door opens. Edwin Schönborn smiles and offers her his hand.

It's a beautiful place, old and high with vaulted ceilings and a white leather sofa. The studio is entirely white. Blum sits down and Edwin Schönborn beams at her. White, regular teeth, expensively dressed, a well-groomed man, handsome, maybe in his midthirties. He offers her coffee. The studio is perfection, one huge room with desks, sofas, makeup tables, and plenty of room to take photographs. Schönborn is the ideal host. A charming man who does nothing to scare Blum off or make her turn against him. Schönborn could be entirely innocent. Why would he, of all people, be the man—the monster—Blum is looking for? He brings the coffee and sits down. They begin talking and everything seems normal. Blum tells lies, Blum improvises, Blum is expecting to go back downstairs empty-handed. Only when the conversation is in full swing does she get the feeling that Schönborn is in fact the man she's looking for. Without knowing it, from one minute to the next he is showing his true colors. He is coming into focus.

"It's great that you found me."

"Yes, indeed. I think I'll be in safe hands here."

"The prerequisite for good nude photos is trust. I'm glad you chose me."

"Your work is very beautiful."

"You're too kind."

"So sensitive. It's as though you put your whole heart into your photographs."

"I give them everything I've got. Every picture ought to be a work of art; it's meant to reflect your soul, show your desire."

"Desire?"

"What you probably like so much about my photographs is the invisible part."

"The invisible part?"

"What can't be seen but nonetheless can be imagined: lust, desire. Showing too much ruins a picture. Destroys its eroticism."

"I quite agree."

"You're a clever woman. And beautiful as well."

"Thank you."

"So these photographs are for your husband?"

"Yes. They're a surprise."

"Underwear?"

"What do you mean?"

"Do you want to wear lingerie in the pictures?"

"No, I'd like to be entirely naked."

"A good idea."

"And I want to be masturbating."

"Wow."

"I'd like you to photograph me while I climax."

"That's what you really want? A picture taken while you masturbate?"

"Exactly."

"Okay. You're on."

"But I just want you to photograph my face."

"What?"

"You said a picture comes to life when it keeps secrets. When
it doesn't show too much. So no breasts, no fingers, no pussy. Just
my face."

"That's very unusual."

"As I said, money is no object."

"Very unusual indeed."

"If you have a problem with that, let's just forget the whole
thing. Maybe it's a bad idea."

"No, it isn't, quite the opposite. It's great."

"You think it's a good idea?"

"A brilliant idea. I must admit I've already had a similar idea
myself."

"Then it's a deal?"

"We're on."

"In the forest?"

"Excuse me?"

"I'd like to do it in the forest. There's a wonderful spot between
Igls and Patsch. I want you to shoot me naked on the mossy ground."

"You want to masturbate out in the forest? Hikers could come
past. Are you sure that's what you want?"

"Yes."

111

"Why?"

"Because it turns me on."

"Whoa."

"I come more easily in public places. I get wild when I know someone might come along. And watch me."

"You filthy bitch."

"What?"

"I'm delighted."

"What did you say?"

"Oh, nothing."

"You called me a filthy bitch."

"I'm sorry. Forgive me. That was very unprofessional."

"Yes, it was, but don't worry about it."

"That's good. That's very good."

"Yes, isn't it? I'm looking forward to this."

"Once again, to avoid any misunderstanding. I'm to photograph your face while you're having an orgasm."

"That's right. Shall we say tomorrow at four in the afternoon? I'll pick you up in my car. We can meet outside the theater. Don't be late."

Blum gets to her feet and leaves. Before he can say anything else she's out in the stairwell. She must stop this, run away, what she said was madness. It simply came over her, she wanted to raise the stakes, see how he would react. She hadn't expected to hit the bull's-eye. Edwin Schönborn. Blum is sure he's the man, and Dunya will recognize his voice, every word he said. That perverted bastard. He'd already had a similar idea himself, had he? Down the steps fast, don't look back, don't react to what he's calling out. Just an offhand *See you tomorrow*, then out into the street. What would have happened if she had stayed? He'd wanted her to stay, he'd touched her arm. She must go to Dunya, fast, she wants to see her face change when she hears his voice. Blum is sure she will see fear in it, fear and horror.

18

She drove through the city in the hearse, an ancient Cadillac Superior from 1972. Her father got it from the States; he wanted to offer his customers something special. Their last drive should be an unusual one. After Hagen's death, Blum had wondered for a long time whether to part with the car, but she had decided against it. It was the jewel in the crown of the undertaker's business and she had grown fond of it. So she wasn't constantly reminded of Hagen, she had the black car repainted. It was now a snow-white hearse. Blum almost screamed at the painter in the garage for asking her, at least ten times, whether she was really sure about the color. A white Cadillac. Stately and elegant. An old lady in a white dress treating her passengers with care. White, not black. Life, not death. Blum wanted to be different, to stand out from her competitors. A white hearse was pure provocation.

In the first two years, before they had the children, Blum and Mark had gone on holiday in that car. They had slept in it on the beach in Sardinia. Blum had made pretty curtains for it herself. They were happy in the white hearse, they had made love and listened to the sea. They had left the trunk open and smoked. She was smoking now. A cigarette in her hand and music on the radio because the dead can't smell a thing. Because Mark is close to her again, because she can sense him, because she wants him to be with her when she meets the man. Blum draws on her cigarette and closes her eyes. At the red light she sees Mark, smiling, taking the cigarette out of her hand and throwing it onto the beach. Kissing her. How warm it is against his skin. Blum hears honking and doesn't want to open her eyes. She doesn't want to, but she must. The light is green again; she is meeting Schönborn in five minutes' time.

Dunya remained silent. She said nothing, only nodded. Blum didn't have to ask more questions or play the conversation to the end. Dunya flinched when his voice came over the little loudspeaker. Edwin Schönborn frightened her and Dunya looked small, everything about her shrunken. *Yes, that's the man who raped me repeatedly. No, there isn't any doubt about it. I'm certain. Yes, it's him, I could pick out his voice in a crowd. His voice and the click of his camera.* Dunya didn't say this, she just lowered her eyes. She was afraid of being punished, of feeling a fist in her face. *Yes, he hit me. Again and again. Everywhere, anywhere it would hurt. His fists, his shoes, his head against mine.* In the girls' room she lay wordless and trembling and Blum hugged her. He had been so easy to find. Blum had been right on target, she had deceived him and challenged him. She had started something, and now she was going to finish it.

Blum throws her cigarette out the window. In three minutes' time she'll be with him, on her own and without a plan. She has no alternative. When she was sitting opposite him in his studio, the idea spontaneously came into her mind to pick him up, take him somewhere, incapacitate him, and bring him back home somehow. It was a crazy idea, she didn't have the faintest idea what she was getting herself into. But Blum resolved to question him, get all he knows out of him, the names of the others, a confession, evidence, a tape recording. He knows who the others are. He knows whether

Mark was murdered, and if so, who did it. She keeps seeing Schönborn in her mind's eye, keeps hearing him say *filthy bitch*. Blum
made him show his true self, unmasked him, saw him switch from
amiable host to disgusting, slobbering pig. A cruel man, with nothing but contempt for the rest of mankind. In two minutes she'll be
with him, he'll be waiting for her outside the State Theater. She
knows he'll be there, he's not going to miss a chance like this.

All afternoon and evening she wondered how to go about it, how
to make him tell her what he knows. How can she knock him out
before he overpowers her? She must be fast, do it while he still
trusts her and is thinking only with his cock. She must get him
into the preparation room, where no one will disturb them. Reza
is away and won't be back until tomorrow. Karl and the children
don't go into that room, so they will be entirely alone. She will talk
to him when he comes back to his senses.

She has looked for a place in this small city where she can knock
him unconscious without being seen. At the railway station, in the
industrial area, in an underground parking garage. She couldn't
make up her mind; she could be seen in any of those places. She
could bring a stone down on his head in the forest where he's supposed to be photographing her, striking him from behind as he
bends to pick something up. In her imagination she hits him so
hard that blood spurts from his head, runs down his forehead in
torrents. She desperately tries to get him onto the stretcher from
the hearse and heave him into the vehicle. He is bloodied and
groaning, she can't manage to lever him up, a jogger comes along
the path. No, that wasn't an option. Schönborn was too heavy, he
must weigh a hundred kilos, she'd have to knock him out in the
car. But she couldn't attack him, because then he'd defend himself,
pull her out of the car and beat her or worse. Knocking him out

with a narcotic is the only possible way. She has Googled it. As do rapists and murderers.

She looked for something that would work fast. Something he would swallow without noticing. Soporifics, something she could get in the next twenty hours, something legal. She has never taken drugs, and doesn't know anyone who does. Many date-rape drugs could be ordered online, but there wasn't time for that; delivery could take up to five days. Blum cursed. She didn't want to postpone the confrontation, she didn't want to give Schönborn time to think; she wanted him thinking only of her pussy. She didn't want him asking questions, getting suspicious. It seemed like a wild goose chase but she searched for a solution all evening like a woman possessed. Then she opened a website that told her the solution was in her garage.

An alloy cleaner. A strong solvent. Butyrolactone, a base for pharmaceuticals and drugs, among them GHB, a date-rape drug. And GBL, a cleaning substance anyone could buy. Sixty euros for a liter. Blum knows that it is in the garage, and has been for years. Hagen bought the solvent over ten years ago, when teenagers had been spraying graffiti on the garden wall. It is right at the back with the winter tires. An industrial cleaner that kept Hagen from having a heart attack and was misused as a party drug, as liquid ecstasy. A high for fourteen cents, the cheapest on the market, and legal too. Blum finishes reading the article and runs down to the garage. The inconspicuous canister stands there with other cleaning products. The problem is solved.

Blum is in the car. A clear liquor in a transparent bottle is on her lap. She has disguised the taste with sugar and Red Bull, she has adulterated it until you can hardly smell the solvent. She was generous with the GBL, however, she has doubled the dose recommended on the Internet; she doesn't want to run any risks. Just one gulp will do it. When he gets into the car she will put the bottle to her lips and pretend to drink. Then she'll say he should have some too. To put them in the mood. She'll hold out the bottle and ask him to drink. She can see Schönborn standing outside the theater, with a black camera case on the ground beside him. In twenty seconds' time the door will open. She will do all she can. For Dunya. In ten seconds' time. For Mark.

19

How unpleasant a man can be. How predictable, when nothing guides him but his instinctive drives: greed, sex, perversion. Blum has taken Schönborn by surprise, but he obliges her by taking the bottle, no questions asked. He drinks from it and grins. Filthy bastard, thinks Blum, smiling sweetly. The liquor in his mouth, the bottle in his hand, and that grin. Before two minutes have passed he is continuing yesterday's conversation, he can't wait, he doesn't want to talk about anything else. First he has to make sure that nothing has changed, she hasn't thought better of it. *Our plan stands?* he asks. Blum nods, she smiles as if by remote control, she forces herself to ignore the fact that there is something suggestive in everything he says. He doesn't even try to hide his lust. *Will it bother you that it turns me on? You masturbating. I can't promise you to keep myself in check.* He laughs out loud and drinks from the bottle again. That dirty laugh; Blum really would like to bring a stone down on his head. She wishes he would keep quiet, stop talking, she doesn't want to spend another second thinking about him taking her photograph. She doesn't want to think about undressing in front of him, so she drives slowly, taking the long way out of the city. She begins talking about Helmut Newton, the only famous photographer whose name she knows. She wants a casual conversation about photography; she wants to slow him down, she must see this through for another ten minutes. By the time they're in the forest he'll have lost consciousness, the GBL will pull the ground out from under his feet. Just ten minutes. Blum smiles, she has almost won when he suddenly asks that question. She hadn't thought of it. Her heart beats fast; why hadn't she thought of it? Blum hates herself. Don't make another mistake, she thinks. As naturally as she can, she replies; lying, without emotion, without hesitation.

"This is a hearse, right?"

"Yes."

"That's cool."

"You get used to it, believe me."

"Why do you drive a hearse?"

"Do you like it?"

"I asked, why do you drive a hearse?"

"Because I think it's cool too. I got it on the Internet."

"Who buys a hearse by choice?"

"I do. I bought it in the States. Apparently President Kennedy was driven from Dallas to Washington in this vehicle. I had to have it."

"You don't have anything to do with funeral parlors, do you?"

"What?"

"Taking dead bodies for a nice drive?"

"Are you crazy?"

"Well, it's the obvious conclusion, isn't it?"

"The only person going for a drive in this car is me. I've come straight from Sardinia. It's really comfortable sleeping in here."

"I'd like to try it myself."

"I can't understand why everyone is so freaked out by the dead."

"I'm not."

"It's only a car. And you can wash a car."

"So it doesn't bother you that dead bodies used to lie in it?"

"Does it bother you?"

"No, it's a great car."

Blum dismisses whatever is going through Schönborn's mind. She drives to Igls, a suburb of Innsbruck, and waits for his head to drop back at last. But his head doesn't drop. Schönborn goes on talking, goes on indulging in tawdry jokes, says how he's looking forward to what is going to happen next. Blum counts the seconds, wonders whether to turn round or stop right there in the middle of Igls. The last thing she wants is to be alone with this man in the forest. She has to come to a decision; they are already on the road between Igls and Patsch, with the forest looming in on both sides. Schönborn asks where she is going to undress. He is wide awake. He is not losing consciousness, he is not dropping off to sleep, he is still very much there. *Not far now*, says Blum. She doesn't know what to do, whether to risk driving on, stopping, getting out of the Cadillac. It can't be much longer now, but all the same, images are tumbling through her head. She sees herself trying to stall, she sees him getting impatient and pushing her to the ground, getting on top of her, tearing down her trousers. Blum sees all that in her mind's eye, but still she turns off the road. She can't help it, she must do it, she drives along the narrow forest path and thinks of Mark. Thinks of him sitting beside her and smiling. Stroking her cheek with his dear fingers. *It will be all right*, he says. She doesn't know yet that this time he is going to be wrong. It is not going to be all right. It is going to be far worse than she imagined.

20

"It's so good of you to come."

"What about the children?"

"Asleep. Come in."

"How are you doing, Blum?"

"Not so well."

"What's the matter?"

"I just don't want to be alone tonight."

"How can I help?"

"I don't know."

"You're shivering. Please tell me how to help you."

"You're here, and that helps."

"Please, Blum. You phoned me. I'm here, and whatever the matter is we can deal with it together."

"Could you hold me close?"

"Now?"

"Lie down on the sofa with me and just hold me close."

"Yes, of course."

"That's the only thing that will help."

"Like this?"

"Yes."

"It will get better, you'll see."

"That's what *he* always used to say."

"Mark?"

"Yes."

"I'm here for you now."

"Thank you, Massimo. And Massimo?"

"What?"

"Could you make love to me?"

"What?"

"Could you?"

"Yes."

Massimo follows her. Blum takes his hand and leads him through the house. Past the bedroom and into Mark's study. Massimo says nothing, he just follows her, does what she wants him to do. He watches as she undresses, then stands naked in front of him. Blum wants to feel something, she wants to take her mind off Schön-born. She lies down on Mark's sofa and tells Massimo to undress too. He hesitates, it is almost as if he doubts her, as if he isn't sure whether Blum is joking. She draws him close, and he lies down beside her. He is quiet, careful, affectionate. Blum takes his hand and places it on her breasts. They don't talk. Blum's eyes are closed. She wants his mouth, his skin, his hands, everything. He is lying on her, kissing her, and she lets him. He is making Schönborn disappear for a little while, everything he has done and everything she has done. Blum embraces Massimo, holds him close, presses him to her. Blum wants her husband's best friend to stay, to warm her, touch her everywhere, she wants him to protect and help her. But no one must know that he is here, lying beside her, holding her in his arms.

For a long time they do not say a word. Blum wants to keep her eyes closed, she doesn't want to open them and see what she has done. She senses that he is inside her, her tongue has disappeared into his mouth. She doesn't want to see his skin, smell him, talk to him. She can't. Whatever she has planned in advance, she won't follow through, won't tell him what has happened. She wouldn't know how to explain it to him, and she doesn't know whether he can help her at all. His hands are tied, he has to keep the rules, there's nothing he can do for her. *The photographer Edwin Schönborn is lying in my cellar, Massimo. Please could you get me out of this? I anesthetized him and abducted him, and he's lying in the preparation room. Come on, Massimo, turn a blind eye and make things all right again. I'm in a fix. Maybe I overreacted, maybe it didn't have to turn out like this, but it's happened now. So you must help me. You know I have children, I can't go to prison now. So please, my dear, see to all this. Thank you, very kind of you.* No, that won't do. Everything has changed. She will take Massimo to the door now. He will get dressed and drive home, and then she will go down to the cellar to see Schönborn. She can't depend on anyone but herself, she will find a way out of her fix, something will occur to her. She will get the ship back on course. Never mind how good his skin feels, never mind whether she hates herself for this, she cannot waste any more time. Blum kisses him and jumps up. *You must go now*, she says. And he asks, *Can I come back?*

21

Three hours earlier. Blum opens the door to the cool room. He is lying on the aluminum table between two caskets. She tied him up like a parcel and left him among the caskets. She was afraid he might come round before she returned; she had to hide him in case Karl or one of the children accidentally wandered in. Now Blum is alone with him.

And there he lies, the monster she has caught. She struck him down, and piled him out of the car like a piece of meat. There's nothing dangerous about him now. She got him into the preparation room unseen, raised him to the aluminum table without any difficulty and wheeled it into the cool room. It was child's play. He is lying between two bodies. Two caskets and Schönborn, at forty-one degrees. She closes the door and leaves him alone. He can wait. Until the children are asleep and she can be with him undisturbed.

But the children weren't sleepy and wouldn't let her go. Blum had to read aloud to them, tell them one story then another. And just one more. While Schönborn slumbered in the refrigerator, Blum was upstairs with Uma and Nela. *Please stay, Mama. We're scared, Mama. Stay until we're asleep. Please.* Even though Blum was impatient to bring Schönborn round and hear what he had to say, she had to stay with the children. Nothing was more important than that. Only when they were lying side by side peacefully, fast asleep, did she return.

How green the moss was. Schönborn waited for her to undress. Everything was out of control, she was panic-stricken, she had overreacted. Blum knew she had to do something. He simply had not gone to sleep, he was full of energy, the solvent didn't seem to affect him at all. So she would have to undress. She didn't want to let things get that far; the game had to end, she must make a decision. She wanted to see him unconscious on the ground; she would ask him questions later and insist on answers. She wanted to know who the others were. Where that cellar was. What had happened to Youn.

She couldn't run away, so she acted quickly. When Schönborn bent down to take something out of the camera case, she struck. The stone had been there, lying on the ground beside her, and it hit Schönborn on the back of the head. The scene was just as she had pictured it, but with less blood. He didn't fall gently asleep, he dropped to the ground with a thud. He fell over forward and collapsed almost without a sound, as if the air had been let out of the monster. He lay there motionless, and without hesitating she began to tie him up. Hands, feet, she rendered him defenseless as she trussed the pig up for roasting.

She got the stretcher out of the hearse and set it up beside him. She pushed with all her might, bracing her body against his. Blum cursed, shouted, spat at him. It was no good; Schönborn was too heavy, and she felt her strength drain away. She had thought it would be easier; in her mind it had been simple enough, but reality was an uneven ground full of roots, and ten meters away from the hearse. Blum was on the point of giving up, leaving him where he was and phoning Massimo. There were tears in her eyes. She spat at him once more, and then she managed to get him on the stretcher. She put one end of it on the loading area of the hearse, raised the other side, and then the bastard disappeared into the vehicle. She loaded him up as best she could, his limbs sprawling and hidden under a blanket. Edwin Schönborn was on his way to the Funerary Institute. Blum was sure that this was the right thing to do, that she had no other option.

She cuddles the children as they fall asleep. Looks at their contented faces before going back to him. Down the stairs, over to the cool room. Over to the door, which she slowly opens. She just stands there for a long time, staring at him. She doesn't move, she only looks. Because she knows she has waited too long, that she ought to have come back sooner to bring him round, to get his circulation going. Blum knew as soon as she opened the cool room door that he would not have survived for over four hours at forty-one degrees under the influence of the drugs and with the head wound. He is like all the other dead bodies she has seen in her life, cold flesh, skin and bones. No heart is beating in the cool room now, there is no sign of life, all she can hear is the engine regulating the temperature. All she sees is his face, his mouth gaping open. Open, but wordless, because he is dead.

Blum doesn't know how long she stood there, as if paralyzed. Perhaps half an hour, perhaps longer. Desperately, she tries to grasp the fact that she is responsible for this. For his silence, for the fact that he is dead. She calls Massimo's number. *Please come to me*, she says. *I'll be with you in twenty minutes*, he replies.

22

It's the middle of the night and Massimo has left. There is blood everywhere. The hydroaspirator sucks and sucks. Blum has opened his stomach cavity and removes the intestines, then puts them in a blue garbage bag. Kidneys, liver, everything she finds goes into the bag. She fixes the aspirator in the cavity with a clamp. Large quantities of blood and other bodily fluids disappear through the tube into the canalization. She opens the chest cavity with diagonal pliers, removes the heart and lungs, and empties the torso before sawing it into small pieces. She cuts through the bones with Hagen's power saw; blood spurts and runs into the tub. She sucks out his flesh and his fat, saws off his horrible head. Without pity or hesitation she takes him apart, cuts him into pieces and packs them up, neatly and hygienically, soaked in a formalin solution. Blum is preserving him; she doesn't want people to notice the smell.

She cleans up until dawn. In a few hours Reza will be back from Bosnia, and there will be two funeral services and two burials this afternoon. He mustn't suspect a thing, she must leave everything the way it was before he left. Blum gets out the caskets in the cool room. The idea had suddenly occurred to her as she was lying naked beside Massimo. Blum saw it all before her eyes while Massimo caressed her. She would put Schönborn's legs, organs, and head into the casket with the old lady. The pieces of his torso and his arms in the casket with the man who died in a mountain-climbing accident. Edwin Schönborn, packed up and preserved, hidden under white blankets with baroque trim. It is the idea that will save her, the only way to escape prison and be there for her girls. She had to do it.

Blum takes the packages and stows them in the caskets. She wedges the body parts between the corpses' legs, ties them in place and hides them. He will be concealed forever. Blum closes the lids of the caskets and screws them down. No one will ever find him; it was a stroke of genius. There's no better place for a corpse than a casket in a graveyard. No one will look for him in the grave of a former teacher or an old lady. No one will suspect a thing. Blum smiles. Exhausted but happy, she pushes the two caskets back into the cool room. Nothing has happened. Everything is all right.

23

No one has noticed a thing. No one knows that Massimo lay naked beside her. That they kissed each other. The children have no idea, and nor does Karl, who was fast asleep in his armchair. Blum covered him up before going back to the children. She lies down beside them, and smiles when they open their eyes. *Mama will look after you. Mama loves you. Now Mama is going to make breakfast for her little mousies.* Blum puts her arms round them and gives them a hug. How innocent they are. How small. How far away Schönborn's body seems. She thinks of the scalpel cutting through his fat.

In a few hours' time he will disappear underground. In a few hours' time she and Reza will drive to the cemetery and see him off with all due form: wreaths, candles, eulogies for the two dead people sharing their caskets with that bastard. Reza has written the eulogies and Blum will deliver them. She will speak solemnly about the lives of the departed, but she will be thinking of Schönborn. She will accompany him to the grave and watch the bearers lower the casket. His legs and his head at two in the afternoon, his torso and his arms at four. Two burials and then Schönborn will be history.

Blum will burn his clothes and go to his studio. In the evening, when the children are asleep, she will unlock the studio with the key she found in his jacket pocket and wipe away any traces, cleaning everything she touched. And she will look for the photographs, for the evidence that she still doesn't have, for the photos telling her what Schönborn couldn't tell her now. Blum must find them and make sure that justice is done. For Mark. For Dunya.

Dunya doesn't ask what Blum is going to do, what her plans are now that she has found the man. Dunya doesn't want to know. When Blum brings up the subject she dismisses it. Blum wants to tell her that she can't do anything, that she doesn't know how to help, that her hands are tied. She wants to lie, but Dunya waves her lies away, puts her forefinger to her lips and shakes her head. *No, please no.* Her fear is in her eyes, she has no more words for it, they have all been spoken. Blum is glad not to have to explain. Dunya is grateful too. She offers to go shopping, she wants to make herself useful. With her head lowered, she takes the money that Blum gives her and leaves the house. Bread for breakfast, eggs, orange juice. Everything seems to be in order; the storm is over.

Bread, eggs, orange juice. Blum is still waiting. The children had some yogurt and then went upstairs to Karl. Blum stays where she is, holding the fort, waiting for Dunya. She has been waiting for two hours now. It doesn't cross her mind that Dunya might not come back. She knows that Dunya feels happy here, that she wants to accept Blum's help. Blum will make sure that she can stay in the country, she'll manage it somehow, she'll pull all the strings she can. But Dunya does not come back.

Dunya has hidden under a stone, thinks Blum, found the most remote cranny of this city. She will go somewhere else, a place where she doesn't know anyone. She wants to be safe, she wants to get away from that voice on Blum's cell phone. With a fifty-euro note in her pocket. Blum stops looking out the window. Dunya has gone. She is only a voice now. A voice telling that story about the cellar. Blum hears it in her head. The story of Ilena, Dunya, and Youn. A photographer, a priest, a huntsman, a chef, a clown. Men in masks. A priest, a huntsman, a chef, a clown. Blum is going to find them.

24

Everything is the same as it always is: the funeral service, the tears, the casket being lowered into the ground. Blum is back at work for the first time in weeks. Reza is glad of that; he's been struggling with a temporary assistant who irritated him. He gives Blum a hug and thanks her. Blum is glad too. He says, *It's good to have you back. This place is nothing without you. Like water without flowers.* Reza is standing there in his dark suit. He drove all night so that he could be back here in time. Blum doesn't know what he was doing in Bosnia; he doesn't talk about that, about anyone who is left or whether he was taking money back to his old home. Reza doesn't say, and Blum doesn't ask. Reza smiles at her while the priest gives the blessing, a small, almost invisible smile. *We'll make it together, we're a team.* She thinks of all the funerals they've arranged together, all the bodies they have prepared, all the burials they have behind them. Reza is a gift. They will wait until all the roses have been dropped into the grave, until all the mourners have said good-bye and the last of them has left the cemetery. They stand there listening to the music, a wind quintet, the chatter of old friends saying good-bye. Blum is looking down at the casket. At Schönborn. And then back at Reza.

He didn't notice a thing, didn't realize that the caskets were heavier than usual. He is the one person who could have been her downfall—he could have suspected, he could have looked inside one of the caskets. But nothing like that has happened. Nothing has been different about him, no doubts, no speculation. Blum's life will stay as it is. It almost seems to be a good thing that Schönborn is dead. Blum senses it. She doesn't think of Mark, she doesn't want to cry, she is thinking only of the parts of a man's torso being lowered into the ground. She killed him. She gave him an overdose, she struck him unconscious, she put him in a refrigerator like a piece of meat. Then she butchered him like a pig.

Blum smiles at Reza; she smiles with her lips, lifting their corners, only very slightly. She feels no guilt or shame. Only that smile playing on her lips, barely perceptible but obvious all the same, and happy. In her mind, Blum is singing, *The filthy pig is dead.* The wind instruments play an old folk song. In her mind, Blum is dancing. She did the right thing and she has no regrets. Only that he can't talk now. Can't tell her who the others are and where she must look for them. She'd do it again without hesitation. She'd do it again. For Dunya. For Mark.

Earth falls into the grave. Blum and Reza watch as the gravedigger fills and seals the hole. It is a delightful sound, the earth on the casket, the sound it makes when it touches the wood, when it covers what is to remain hidden. No one will ever open that grave again, no one will look for Schönborn down there. Blum's mind is still dancing, rejoicing in the knowledge that the nightmare has a happy ending. They stay until the end, until the grave is only a mound of earth decorated by flowers. Only then do they go, Reza and Blum, to a bar, where they sit drinking in easy companionship. A couple of beers, half an hour. Then she will go; she will embrace Reza and go. *There's something else I have to do*, she will say. Reza will nod. Blum will walk to the Old Town, she will unlock the door of the building and go upstairs, she will open the studio door and lock it again on the inside. She will search everywhere, every nook and cranny, every hard disk, she will not stop until she has found the photos. Portraits of Ilena, of Dunya, of Youn. She will be wearing gloves, she will wipe everything she touched two days ago, no trace of her will be discovered when he is reported missing. She will delete their first meeting from his diary if he entered it. Blum will make no mistakes; she will leave unseen with the photographs, she will retreat into Mark's study to look at the pictures. She will see what went on in that cellar. She will look into their faces, and she will cry over them, she knows that. She will hate those men more with every portrait she sees. Blum will finish her beer now, get up and embrace Reza. She will walk to the Old Town and unlock the door. *There's something else I have to do.*

25

Karl is better now that he has let the children back into his life. He spends a lot of time with them. The children are like a balm. He and Blum agree on that as they sit side by side on the garden bench, watching them play. Every day, although the girls don't know it, they keep the boat from capsizing, they make sure that their mother gets up and goes out into the day, that Karl doesn't lie down forever. Mark lives on in their little faces. That thought stops them from giving up.

"You're working again. That's good."

"Thank you for helping me with the children, Karl."

"It's the children who help me."

"What would I do without you?"

"Don't say that. It's the other way around. What would *I* do without *you*? If you hadn't asked me to live here, I'd be dying slowly in a nursing home."

"Don't talk like that."

"You know I'm right, Blum."

"You belong to us and we love you, Karl."

"And who loves you?"

"The three of you."

"But there's something on your mind."

"You mustn't worry, Karl. I'm fine."

"There is something. I know you. It's to do with that woman."

"Oh, Karl."

"I know I'm right."

"Once a cop . . ."

"What is it about her? She left without saying good-bye."

"So? Karl, everything's just fine. Dunya is a friend of mine from the past. She always came and went as she pleased."

"Nonsense."

"What do you mean, nonsense?"

"She's no friend of yours. You hardly know her."

"Please drop the subject, Karl."

"I can help you."

"You can and do help me by looking after the children. I can manage everything else on my own."

"There's something wrong. I can sense it."

Blum can imagine Karl as he was before the tick made an old man of him. Unyielding, a bloodsucker himself, the sort who never stops asking questions until the truth comes to light. *He was a good police officer*, Mark said, he learned all he knew from him. His instinct, his persistence. But she's not going to tell Karl a thing, she won't confide in him, won't put him in danger. Even though Blum knows that he would never judge her or give her away, she bites her tongue. Saying nothing, she leaves him with his dark presentiments. Blum takes his hand and presses it. Karl knows she's stubborn; he knows she isn't going to tell him a thing. He's known her long enough. He has come to love her for all that she is and all that she isn't. She will not tell him that she has killed a man, cut him into pieces and buried him. She isn't going to tell him that the man was probably Mark's murderer. That there are four more of them out there. She won't tell him any of that. Only their intertwined fingers matter. Blum's hand in his must be enough. Karl must trust her.

How glad she is that he's there. While she goes on investigating, like a woman possessed, looking for those men, Karl cooks for the children, puts them to bed, reads aloud to them. Those men must be somewhere, and somehow or other Blum will find them. Even though she knows less than nothing, she will run them to ground and make them talk. All four of them. But she doesn't know where to begin. Men between thirty and sixty, inconspicuous and friendly, no one in the world would think for a moment that they could do something so perverted. White sheep innocently grazing in a meadow, probably leading a perfectly normal life, probably quite close to Blum. Respectable citizens like Schönborn. Men of good repute, psychopaths, murderers. By now Blum is convinced that they are responsible for Mark's death. There can be no doubt about it, everything fits.

26

The man in the suit could be in his midfifties. Johannes Schönborn, Edwin's father, the provincial government deputy, former
owner of the hotel in Sölden. Blum simply went to the government building, then up to the second floor, where she asked to
see him. No appointment was available, she was told, for another
five weeks. She thanked the man and waited outside Schönborn's
office. For an hour she stared at the picture hanging on the wall:
a woman with the head of a stag, breasts, and a pair of antlers. It
was just Blum and the woman with the stag's head. Schönborn
was the only one who could tell her the truth about the presumed
brothel in the "wellness" area of the hotel, about potential clients,
about Dunya, Youn, and Ilena. He must know something, he must
have something to do with it. So she followed him when he left
his office. He went to a restaurant; she sat down at the bar and
observed him. It was lucky that he was eating alone, that the chair
opposite him was vacant, was waiting just for her.

Blum is surprised by the man's aura of calm, the composure with
which he continues to eat. It seems almost as if he found her
appearance a welcome diversion. A man with nothing to fear, a
man who feels safe, who is aware of his power and prepared to
use it.

"I have to ask you about your brothel."

"You have to what?"

"Ask you about your brothel. In the Annenhof hotel, remember?"

"I'm not entirely sure that I understand you correctly."

"Yes, you do."

"I would like to eat my lunch in peace."

"That's fine by me, so long as you tell me what made you do it."

"You can't be serious?"

"Oh yes, I am."

"What in the world are you thinking? You interrupt my meal, and you have the impertinence to spoil my appetite with groundless accusations."

"As I said, you're welcome to go on eating."

"Have we met?"

"No, but I could tell everyone here that I used to work for you."

"What do you mean?"

"In your wellness center. I could tell them all that I procured for you. I could make quite a scene of it, and I'm sure some of them would believe me. I'm good at that sort of thing."

"Why would you do a thing like that?"

"Because I'd like to know whether that brothel was part of your hotel."

"How entertaining you are."

"Am I?"

"Very amusing, yes. By the way, the pasta here is excellent. You ought to try it."

"You haven't answered my question."

"There was no such brothel. Never."

"Nonsense."

"The ladies gave massages, that was all. Classic back massages, sound massages, lymph drainage, underwater pressure jet massages, Ayurvedic and hot-stone massages, the full range. They were much appreciated by our guests."

"The clients in the brothel, you mean."

"Guests, young lady, satisfied guests. Why, even the village pastor was a regular guest of ours."

"The pastor?"

"Yes, that speaks for itself, don't you agree? A man of God gave the whole enterprise his blessing. He has trouble with slipped disks, poor man. The ladies helped him a great deal. That was all, it was perfectly aboveboard."

"So you left the pastor satisfied too?"

"Yes, he's a very good man, and it looks as if he'll be the next bishop."

"And he was one of your regular guests?"

"Yes again, and now I trust that I have answered all your questions and we can enjoy a glass of wine together."

"I'll be happy to join you."

"By the way, what makes you think there was something wrong with the hotel all that time ago? And why now, after so many years? Why do you take any interest in this tedious subject?"

"You're a huntsman, aren't you?"

"What if I am?"

"Five men enjoying themselves."

"What?"

"With Ilena, Dunya, and Youn."

"I have no idea what you're talking about, but I'm always happy to talk to my constituents, particularly when they're as pretty as you."

"Are you a rapist?"

"I beg your pardon?"

"Are you one of the five men?"

"Are you drunk? What on earth are you talking about?"

"I'm talking about abduction, unlawful imprisonment, assault, rape. And murder."

"Enough. I think you'd better leave."

"Father and son. Perhaps the two of you were having your fun together."

"What about my son? What's all this about?"

Blum turns and leaves without another word or glance. She simply walks away, with everything that he has said ringing in her ears. And everything that he hasn't. He didn't know what she was talking about, he'd never heard the names Ilena, Dunya, and Youn before. He was surprised. He racked his brain and found nothing, his astonishment was genuine. And so were his denials about the brothel. How confidently he twists reality, extinguishes the past. Only massages. Massages for the pastor. How absurd.

His mention of the pastor is a bonus. A gift that someone has handed her, and all she has to do is open it. Remove the ribbon, crumple up the wrapping paper. A present that Johannes Schönborn has given her without knowing the avalanche he has set in motion. Blum pictures the randy priest punishing Dunya for her sins. A man of God in the brothel, a man of God in a cellar somewhere in hell. The son of the house is a photographer. A priest is a regular client. Blum knows him. She has met him at funerals, she knows his face, she knows how he speaks and moves. She sees him in her mind's eye.

His name is Herbert Jaunig. He wears a kindly expression as he delivers the eulogy. As he shakes hands with the bereaved. As he rapes Youn. As he drags the girls out of their cages to whip them. Everything that Blum has heard comes back to her. Every word that

Dunya told her, every little detail. He would punish Dunya for her sins, bringing his belt down on her back again and again, the belt buckle digging into her skin, screams echoing in the cellar. The way he quotes the Bible as he ties the boy down on the table. The way he seizes Youn by the hair and jerks his head up as he thrusts into him, the pastor's sanctified prick absolving the boy of his sins as it roots around inside him. The savior bringing those three lost souls back to the path of righteousness, the future bishop lovingly tending to his flock. Blow by blow, thrust after thrust. Punishment for the lascivious behavior of his victims, his fist coming down on the boy's back so hard that it almost drives the breath out of him. Dunya sits in her cage watching and can do nothing to help.

Blum leaves the restaurant. Not for a second does she doubt the existence of that brothel in the Annenhof. She doesn't believe that the pastor went there only for massages. He must have been an associate of Edwin Schönborn. She has no doubt about it, and no pity. She sees only the pastor before her eyes, only the photos that Edwin Schönborn took. Again and again those faces; she read those faces all night long, in the photos that she found in Schönborn's studio. In an unlocked drawer, neatly sorted and stacked. Blum couldn't stop looking at them: those eyes, the gaping mouths, the horror and emptiness on their faces. She has seen everything that Herbert Jaunig has done. All that he must answer for now. The good priest, one of the most popular in the country. Blum will make him talk.

27

Massimo wants to touch her again, hold her close. He says so quietly. He is sitting beside her at the dining table, and the children are playing on the floor. It is suppertime. Massimo simply dropped by, he wants to be there for her. His helpfulness, his concern, his warm hand touching her. *I need time. I don't know if that was wise of me, I was so lonely. I'm grateful to you, Massimo. Please let's take things slowly. I have to think, Massimo. You're wonderful, but all the same it was wrong, because of Mark. You know that. Forgive me.* She says these things without words, only with the touch of her fingertips. They do the talking, caress him, console him. Because she knows he wants more. He wants to be with her, day and night. But she can't, not yet. She is afraid of it, she doesn't want the children or Karl to see that the family friend has suddenly come between them. Blum would like to strip this closeness away now, be rid of it. It is suddenly burdensome to have him there, wanting something from her. She must tell him he should go, say she would rather he call before coming. Blum knows that she has made a mistake, she was thinking only of herself; she knows she will hurt him if she tells him to go away. She knows that, and his fingers can feel it. They reach for her, longing, crying out. *Not now, Massimo, please. Please give me time.* She looks at him, asking him to go. *I have to put the children to bed. I'll call, thank you, you're an angel.* She takes him to

151

the door, embraces him, feels his warmth. But then she puts the brakes on, draws away from him and closes the door. She is alone again with the children. She doesn't want any other man, only Mark.

She stands in the bathroom for two minutes. She won't let herself cry. She has to brush the children's teeth, play with them, be a good mother, read them a bedtime story. She must be there for them, soothe her guilty conscience for letting Karl take on too much. But she can't unsee what she's seen, everything that has cast her life into confusion for the past five weeks. It's there, it occupies every minute of her waking hours. When the girls are asleep, when they're awake. She thinks of Dunya, of the Schönborns, of the priest. While she's getting the girls into their pajamas, while she reads them the story of the dancing horse, while she lies in the dark beside them humming a tune. Because it's like a fever. That feeling, the rage, the certainty that Mark might still have been alive. Everything is in movement, everything will change.

But morning follows night, and with it her everyday routine. Funerals, Reza, the children, laying out bodies, preparing them, the tears of their relations. And the same questions all the time. How will she go about it? How will she overpower him? Where can she get him on his own? She thinks of nothing but Herbert Jaunig for days on end. She reads everything she can find about him on the Internet. She finds out where he lives, how he lives. She watches him, follows him. She watches him saying mass in the cathedral, raising his hands to break the bread, drinking the wine from a golden goblet. A priest like any other, a man of God.

Hagen used to take her to church every Sunday. And every Sunday Blum hoped that the man in the cassock would help her. She had told him that she didn't want to live anymore. She was eight years old. She had been alone with him one afternoon in the confessional, safe and sad. She had told him that she couldn't breathe anymore, that she wanted a cuddle. An eight-year-old girl summoning up all her courage, trying to put her unhappiness into words, begging for help. Begging the man in the cassock who kept talking about brotherly love and mercy. Blum had cried. She remembers whimpering very quietly. He had heard her, and told her to stop that. His voice through the grating hadn't done anything to make it better. Instead of taking her in his arms he had given her his prescription for happiness. Two Our Fathers and a Hail Mary. Three prayers for a happy childhood. A child who wanted to die, and a man of God.

Every Sunday she had hoped that he would take her aside, that he would remember what she had told him so often. Blum had believed for a long time that he could help her because Jesus was a good man, because Blum had been stupid enough to believe that. Twenty-four years later she stands at the very back of the church looking at the altar, watching without emotion as Herbert Jaunig gives the blessing, spreading wide his arms and promising heaven. A hypocrite, a play-actor, not a man of God. Not Jesus, just a man in his midfifties. Not a lamb but a wolf.

28

"Blum?"

"Yes?"

"How much longer?"

"Not long. I can hear someone moving about. We must wait until the staff have gone home."

"Did I ever tell you you're crazy?"

"Yes, you did. But that won't get you anywhere. We must go through with it now."

"But you know I'm a police officer."

"Don't get so antsy, darling."

"We could at least open the champagne."

"We're sitting in a closet, Mark."

"So? Is it against the rules to drink champagne in a closet?"

"We wanted to celebrate in the mattress department."

"You wanted to."

"Because you don't want a water bed. What else could I do?"

"Correct, I'm not in favor of a water bed, and that's why we're spending the night in a furniture shop."

"Exactly."

"If they catch us it could be very awkward for me, you know."

"Then don't be so impatient."

"I want to drink a toast with you here and now."

"We have to wait."

"Okay, then I want to kiss you while we wait."

"Not yet."

"Then when?"

"Soon."

"But I want to kiss you now, not later, Blum."

"Do you really, really want to kiss me now?"

"Yes."

"Then come with me."

Blum opened the closet door and ran, ran on tiptoe through the furniture store. Hand in hand with Mark, upstairs. To the mattress studio, the water bed. They sank into it, giggling and embracing, then kissed. It was their wedding day, six years before. When she thinks of it, the memory still makes her tingle. She can see it in her mind's eye—the face of the night watchman who suddenly appeared. The flashlight that came on, the beam of light shining on their bodies. Two lovers in each other's arms, lying calmly on a water bed. Instead of jumping to their feet they simply looked up and past the watchman's uniform to his face. No one said a thing, the night watchman didn't move. Mark and Blum were smiling, there was no resistance. They gave themselves up and didn't try to run away, but lay in their embrace, waiting to see how he reacted. The night watchman, the strong arm of the law. They were expecting the worst, but the worst didn't happen. Instead of threatening them, exerting his authority over them, the night watchman grinned and politely informed them that the furniture shop was closed. Then he escorted them to the exit, just like that.

In the parking lot outside the furniture store they could hardly believe what had happened. To think that they'd been caught and there were no consequences! Only their laughter ringing out over the empty lot. Mark opened the champagne and Blum drank out of the bottle as they sat in the car, because it had begun to snow. Six years ago, in the little Polo where Blum was now waiting for Jaunig. Drinking champagne, holding hands, laughing until the bottle was empty. For a long time they sat in the car, watching the snowflakes fall, until the windshield was white, until they were alone. Mark and Blum, safe under a blanket of snow.

Blum is alone now. There is no snow on the windshield. The seat beside her is empty. It is summer, and what happened then is only a lovely, painful memory. Blum waits for Jaunig to come up the slope. She knows he will soon be running this way, it won't be long now. He's done that for the last four days, always at the same time. She has waited for him outside the presbytery. Every evening he has arrived in the forecourt of the cathedral in his gray tracksuit and begun to run. Out of the Old Town just before darkness fell. Over the bridge of the River Inn, along Höttingergasse and up to the forest.

Blum waits. She keeps looking in the rearview mirror, where she sees her face, her eyes. She thinks how Mark always told her that she had an unhappy mouth; it showed when she was sad or tired. She thinks of all the good things that Mark brought. How he had replaced her past.

Blum firmly believes he will come. She knows he will come. She has planned it all. She needed two days on her own, she said, two days at the seaside. *Please, Karl, look after everything. I'm so grateful to you, Karl.* She promised to bring the children something back, seashells and sand. She hugged Karl. Then she drank a glass of wine in the kitchen. The children were playing with modeling clay, and she decided on the next step, on what will happen when Herbert

Jaunig appears at the end of the path. She remembers, with all her might, everything that isn't here now, everything beautiful. She remembers Mark. It helps her justify what is about to happen.

The man of God comes, running towards Blum, who is ready to turn the key in the ignition. He can see the little car beside the path. He thinks nothing of it, he runs on. Until he reaches her, until she turns the key, about to step on the gas. Another twenty seconds. She must do it. Now, go!

She feels the car striking his body as the future bishop falls to the ground. She has only a brief glimpse of his horrified face; she doesn't hesitate for a second, she runs him over, breaking bones. Pitilessly, Blum brakes and reverses. She must work fast, she must drag him into the car, force him into the trunk, wrestle with his legs, his arms, his torso. She jumps out of the car and uses all her strength to push, haul, and lift the priest into the small trunk. He is only a mass of flesh and bones. She ignores the pain he must be feeling. She ties him up with duct tape, gags and binds him. An accident, she thinks. Just an unfortunate accident. Breathlessly, she slams down the cover of the trunk, gets back into the car, and drives away. In six hours' time she will be in Trieste. In six hours' time she will talk to him. If he's still alive then.

There are no traffic checks along the highway. She takes care not to attract attention; she has a full tank and doesn't need to stop. She feels no pity for the priest. She doesn't hear him groaning, doesn't hear any noises coming from the car trunk. The sound of the engine drowns them out. The road runs through the Italian countryside, all of it familiar, every service station that she passes, the road signs at the exits. Blum and Jaunig are on their way to the sea. There is plenty of time to think, plenty of time to get accustomed to the situation, to the fact that she has killed before, and may kill again. She remembers that TV series.

Dexter. Mark loved it. He would sit in his study watching it for hours on end, watching a forensic scientist administering his own ideas of justice. Taking villains out of circulation, liberating the world from scum. Mark loved all seven seasons; he kept trying to persuade Blum to join him in the world of the serial murderer. Blum always laughed at him. She didn't understand how Mark could think that anything on that show was remotely like reality. *Nonsense*, she said, lying down beside him on the sofa. It was all nonsense, so far-fetched, a man striking out on his own against the villains who had fallen through the net. A man of the law making sure that justice is done because no one else will. It was a fable of revenge, unrealistic and pointless. All the same, Blum lay there beside him, watching the man on the screen pinning his victims down on a table with plastic wrap. Plunging a knife into their hearts, then chopping them up and throwing the parts into the sea. It made Blum laugh. At Mark, and at Dexter. Dexter was nothing more than a murderer. She tried to get Mark to see that, but he defended Dexter to the hilt, even though he was a police officer himself.

Just before reaching Verona, Blum smiles. She has abducted a man, just like Mark's hero, she has chopped him into pieces and put the pieces in caskets. She thinks of the hearse, the Funerary Institute, the cold room, the preparation room. Perfect conditions. Blum's screenplay is better.

Blum drives on. She is composed, almost indifferent. She knows the peace that comes from within, even when your world has been turned upside down. She drives straight on. Just as she steered the boat so long ago. In the sunlight, eight years before. There's nothing to stop her now. It's the middle of the night, and Trieste lies just ahead. Herbert Jaunig is still alive. If she drives really slowly she can hear his groans, and the wheels passing over the asphalt. The sound of the wind, the car engine, and that muffled bellowing, distorted by the gag. Pain, despair, fear. Blum drives on without pity. He is still breathing, he can speak, and he will speak. They're nearly there. Just down the winding roads to the harbor. The familiar pier, the Lanterna di Trieste, the old yacht, the sea.

29

She slams the cover of the trunk down on his head, hitting Jaunig for the second time. He tries to sit up and shout for help, but Blum strikes again. She isn't going to waste a second; she has parked the car close to the boat. Jaunig doesn't have a chance, there's no one there to help him, no one to prevent Blum from dragging him out of the car trunk and onto the yacht. Never mind how heavy he is, never mind how difficult the task is and how quickly it has to be done, Blum just gets on with it, because someone could come along at any moment. Jaunig has wet himself. He is just a piece of meat that she tips straight down into the mess area of the cabin, where they ate; he falls directly on the table. Unconscious in the bowels of the boat, defenseless as a baby.

Blum parks the car, unfastens the rope, and is ready to cast off in less than ten minutes. She wants to leave the harbor as quickly as she can, and be alone with him when he comes round. She ties him down to the table and pours gasoline over him. Then she starts the engine and steers the large boat carefully away from the pier. How good and familiar the world smells. Down below, Jaunig is coming to his senses. Overhead, the night sky is moving slowly towards day. Wonderful, she thinks, taking a long, deep breath. Italy.

She is out on the water now, far away from everyone. She feels free, even now, never mind what happens next. There is nothing but blue water, the waves, the salt on her skin. Maybe the sun will shine today, maybe it will rain. Never mind how the day turns out, Jaunig will be silenced. The whimpering and groaning will soon die away. She stays on deck a little while longer, steering the boat past the breakwaters, until she is thirteen miles out in the open sea. Then she turns the engine off and goes down below. She tells him to stop kicking up such a fuss or she'll set him on fire. Then she tears the sticky tape off his mouth. He is in great pain, she can see, but he says nothing. He is trembling all over, but he tries to keep himself under control. He looks at Blum, he can't move so much as an inch. Blum stands beside him with a lighter in her hand.

"If you lie to me I shall set you on fire."

"My legs. I can't move them. You must help me."

"Did you understand what I said?"

"You must get me to a hospital."

"You are going to tell me everything."

"What do you want from me? This is madness. Let me go. Please."

"I want to know who the other three men are. Where I can find them, their names."

"I need painkillers."

"Your pain is of no importance now."

"For God's sake, put that lighter away."

"There were five of you. After Edwin Schönborn, that leaves three other men."

"What are you talking about?"

"Don't say the wrong thing, because you aren't going to get a second chance."

"I am a priest."

"That didn't help the girls and the boy."

"We can talk about that later. It's not what you think."

"No, it's worse, much worse, and you know it."

"I don't know who those men are. They wore masks. I have no idea who the others are. You must believe me."

"Why are you lying?"

"I'm not lying."

"None of them will help you now."

"Do you want money? The diocese will set it all up. I can get you as much money as you want."

"You think you can go back to your cathedral and do good works, just as if nothing had happened?"

"I never did anything else. You must believe me."

"Dunya. Ilena. Youn."

"They were lost souls. I was caring for their souls, don't you understand? You must put that lighter away now and untie me."

"What about the boy? What did you and the others do to him?"

"I can help you. You can still go back. It doesn't all have to end like this. God will forgive you, believe me. His mercy is infinite."

"Hold your damn tongue."

"I can see that you're unhappy, you have strayed, you can't find your way back to the path of righteousness. You are helpless and desperate, let me stand by you. Please. Untie me."

"I was very happy once."

"You will be happy again. But only if you put that lighter down. What you're doing won't help anyone."

"My happiness is dead."

"I suggest we pray together. Whatever has happened to you, you can leave it behind you. Look at me. You have run me over, my bones are broken. You've put me in the trunk of a car, hit me, and poured gasoline over me. And yet I am ready to see the goodness in you. God's help enables us to bear any pain."

"The police officer you and your friends ran over was my husband."

"I'm really sorry. But every loss can be overcome. You must look forward again, let life in once more."

"Yes, you're right about that."

The things he says. The things he doesn't say. Asking anything else is pointless; he'd rather die than talk. Blum knows that. So she sets him on fire. Slowly and calmly she leans forward and holds the lighter to his clothes. As if she were lighting a candle, she sets the priest on fire, even if her reason tells her what she is doing is madness. She sees flames. The priest's wide, staring eyes. The way he roars, abuses her. The wolf is trying to savage her with words. Jaunig begins to burn.

Slowly, Blum gets to her feet and climbs up on deck. She doesn't turn to look back, she no longer hears his screams. She watches the sky grow gradually lighter. She doesn't see Jaunig trying to tear himself free, tossing desperately back and forth, screaming for his life, trying to protect his face. She doesn't see his burning clothes, his hair, his skin, she just stands there looking at the morning sky. For two long minutes, there is nothing but Blum and daybreak. Everything in her is still. She inhales the sea air, breathing deeply in and out. Then she goes below once more.

The foam from the fire extinguishers has preserved the boat from major damage. She protected everything round him, distributing the contents of three fire extinguishers on the floor and seats of the cabin. She tied Jaunig so tightly to the table that the flames remained under control, consuming only him. Blum has done it all exactly right. She acts very fast now. She throws blankets over Jaunig to put out the flames. There is smoke and soot everywhere, the mess looks like purgatory. Jaunig lies on the table before her. Jaunig is no longer breathing. The good Lord failed to come to his aid.

Blum surveys the scene. The boat has suffered damage to the cabin floor, upholstery and ceiling, and the mast. All the same, she smiles. She'll have the cabin renovated. For years she's been wanting to drive the spirit of Herta and Hagen out of the boat, change it to her taste. Now is the time and Jaunig has given her a reason. She will have it entirely refurnished in the spring and throw away the old fixtures and fittings. She will fulfill a dream, go sailing with the children in May. Everything she can see will be gone. There'll be nothing to remind her of Jaunig.

30

Blum is keeping watch. She has been sitting on the bench in front of the cathedral for over two hours, waiting. It is early morning, and she has driven all through the night, from Trieste to Innsbruck in four hours, twenty-four minutes. She wanted to get back to her children, to her family, to be rid of Jaunig at long last. So far no one has seen the plastic bag from the supermarket. The bag doesn't look right here, it ought to attract attention. It cries out to be taken down from the cathedral door where Blum hung it. For two hours, she has been waiting for something to happen; for someone to find it.

Yesterday Blum was still at sea. It was a sunny day, a wonderful day. Exhausted and happy, she let the boat drift on the water. She had done the right thing. Jaunig was dead. Blum hasn't often had burnt bodies on her preparation table, only a few times in her life. She went down to the cabin and stared at him, fascinated to see what damage the fire had done in just two minutes. The fire had taken hold everywhere his body was exposed, disfiguring his face, his hands.

Blum cut the dead priest's head off. It had all gone according to plan; she put a bucket under the table and hacked at his neck with an ax until the head came away. She caught his blood in a bucket. Then she got rid of the body and cleaned up the blood. It was only a small cabin fire, an accident in the mess area, a candle she had forgotten to blow out. Blum scrubbed and scoured the soot on the cabin ceiling, the charred table. It almost looked as if nothing had happened. Then she put Jaunig's head in a plastic bag and threw his body to the sharks.

It was Mark who had told her about them. Had told her there really were sharks off the coast of Trieste, and they came from the open sea into land with the freighters. These sharks were a threat to tourists, and were kept away from the beaches by gratings. But they swam directly under the point where Blum was letting her boat drift; the sea was twenty-four meters deep here. It was a good resting place for Jaunig's body, though not his head.

Blum doesn't want him to disappear and be forgotten. She wants people to know that this man has done something so terrible he had to die for it. Blum wants to flush the toads out of the undergrowth, scare them out of cover, give them a fright. Something will happen, she thinks, a sign of what she should do next. Jaunig is dead. He refused to confess and that was a sin. Blum has learned nothing except that Jaunig was one of them, and had known about Mark's death. Had been amused by it. *Every loss can be overcome. You must look forward again, let life in once more.* Blum can still hear his words, and then the click of her lighter.

Twelve hours ago, she was still at sea. Now she is staring at the bag. She is sitting under a tree, fifty meters from Jaunig's head. You wouldn't notice her at first glance; she is at home in this peaceful scene: the cathedral, the fountain, and a woman reading a book in the morning air. A woman waiting for someone to take the head out of the plastic bag.

31

A man of eighty-four has hanged himself. Reza and Blum have cut him down from the roof rafter, and now he is lying in the cool room. Nela is painting a picture, Uma has an upset tummy. Now it is mid-September and everyday life has taken over. Massimo has phoned several times. Some teenagers, drunk, have found Herbert Jaunig's head, and the papers are full of it. At first the teenagers thought the thing in the plastic bag was a soccer ball. Blum watched as they tipped it out of the bag and kicked the priest's head. She saw them freeze; one of them threw up. Now she is reading all about it in the paper. Father Herbert Jaunig has been brutally murdered and beheaded. And the world doesn't know what to make of it.

Blum is sitting at the breakfast table with the children. There's a photo in the paper of the cathedral forecourt, cordoned off with police tape. She holds a slice of bread and homemade jam, remembering yesterday. Uma and Nela are undressing, running around the apartment with nothing on. *You get undressed too, Mama, please.* Blum eats her bread and jam. She looks at the girls. How carefree they are, how untroubled. There are moments when they don't think of their father, when they act as if nothing has happened. But still, they have lost Mark; that is their reality. The head of the man expected to become bishop is only a newspaper story, a crime that shakes this little provincial city, a topic on which the public can wax indignant. But, to them, it is nothing more than that. Blum smiles, and helps herself to another slice of bread and jam.

She doesn't know what will happen now. Jaunig's head will probably be embalmed or frozen, they'll store it in the Forensic Medicine department and search frantically for his body. The church will call for a funeral. But Jaunig's head will stay in the freezer for months, even years. His body won't be found because the sharks have eaten every last morsel. Nothing will lead back to the cellar or to Blum. No one believed Dunya; they said her story had been dreamt up for the benefit of the police. Nothing will emerge from police investigations. His friends and acquaintances will be questioned, but none of them will be proved guilty. The real murderer will remain unknown.

Blum will stay a little longer, watching the children, and then Karl will take over while she and Reza attend to their corpse, the hanged man. Hagen used to say: work early in the day keeps troubles away. Hagen and Herta. Schönborn. Jaunig. Four people are dead. Blum breathes deeply in and out. She has a clear conscience, she'd do it all again. She'd even sleep with Massimo. He was there when she needed him. Still, when the phone rings and she sees his name on the display, she wonders whether to pick up. This is the fifth time he's called. Her hesitation is brief; then she hears his voice.

"Where've you been?"
"At sea."
"Why?"
"Massimo, please don't do this."
"I miss you."

"Don't you have enough to keep your mind off that at work? It sounds as though all hell has broken loose."

"You're right about that."

"What exactly happened?"

"I don't know, Blum, but it's pretty perverted."

"I hear they beheaded him."

"Looks like it."

"Who'd do a thing like that?"

"I wish I knew."

"And who, for God's sake, wants to murder a priest?"

"That's what I'm going to find out."

"Make sure you do."

"I could come round and see you after work."

"Where are you?"

"In the presbytery."

"How long for?"

"Oh, a long time."

"I'll come and find you."

"You can't, Blum, I have to work."

"Just for a moment, I just want to see you."

"No."

"Please."

"Well . . . it's number five, Domplatz. Phone me when you get here."

"What would I do without you?"

32

Massimo doesn't send her away from the apartment that was Jaunig's presbytery. And Blum wants to know what's going on there, whether anything might lead to Dunya, might give her away. She told Massimo that she misses him. Needs him. Then she got straight into her car. He took her briefly in his arms. Blum wanders round Jaunig's apartment among men in white overalls. She knows many of the police officers here; they've come to barbecues in her garden. She said she had to speak to Massimo, and they let her in at once. She is familiar with the work of crime scene investigators. The number of bodies she has collected for forensics is too high to count. The men in white overalls are looking for traces, taking fingerprints and DNA samples. The whole department is in action, packing up everything that might provide a clue. But they don't know what they are looking for, she can tell that from Massimo's face. It is a mystery to them. A priest who has become a murder victim, a man with no enemies, a man who gave himself to the service of God. Who would want to harm him, who would have any reason to burn and behead him then hang his head on the cathedral door like a memento? All they can do is look for leads, talk to his friends and acquaintances, investigate his life, search for inconsistencies. Guessing nothing untoward, they go through the apartment. Guessing nothing untoward, Massimo kisses her on both cheeks, right then left. *Let's go and have a quick drink at the wine bar,* he says. *Please let me stay a little longer,* she says.

Blum manages to persuade him. She wants to stay because of Mark, she says. She likes to remember him by the work he did. She sees him in her mind's eye. Normally he'd have been here, putting evidence in bags, taking fingerprints. Since Jaunig was found yesterday morning Mark would have been working steadily, just like Massimo is now. This case is at the forefront of everyone's mind: the church, the politicians, and the congregation are all demanding answers. Blum hears them expressing their horror, their fear of a monster in their midst. Jaunig has been executed, and they are looking for the judge who sentenced him to death. They are looking for Blum.

She sits inconspicuously at Jaunig's desk. *We'll soon be finished here,* says Massimo. Blum's eyes wander round the room, she sees everything that he saw. Herbert Jaunig will never sit here again, he'll never take a book off that shelf again, never pray again. Never rape again. Blum has made sure of that. She sits there, satisfied, watching. It was right that she didn't ask Massimo for help. How could he have helped her? He'd have had to go against all his beliefs, lie for her, and cover up a crime. She can't and doesn't want to make him do that. This is her story, not his. She started it and she will see it through to the end.

After ten minutes Massimo asks her to leave. He accompanies her down the stairs, puts his arms around her, and kisses her greedily. His lips are suddenly on hers, his tongue is in her mouth, his body is very close. Blum lets it happen. She doesn't feel a thing. It's only his desire, his hands on her, him whispering what he wants. How difficult it is for her to push him away, tell him she can't, he must understand that she is thinking only of Mark. But she is thinking of Jaunig too. Of the men who took Mark away from her, tore him and his tenderness away. She won't stop looking, she will find them.

The clown, the cook, the huntsman.

33

He grabbed her by the arm just after she had said good-bye to Massimo. She wanted to sit in the wine bar for a moment and think. About the kiss. About what she had seen in the priest's apartment. She had embraced Massimo, then gone into the wine bar and ordered a glass of white. A glass of wine before turning her attention to the next man she would take out, her next corpse. She had just taken the first sip of wine when Schönborn was there beside her. His fleshy fingers were grabbing her forearm, announcing that he meant business.

"What have you done to my son?"

"I beg your pardon?"

"He's disappeared, I haven't been able to reach him for days. I want to know what's going on."

"If you touch me again I'll scream."

"I want to know where my son is."

"I don't know your son."

"If you don't tell me what you know, you'll be sorry."

"Are you threatening me?"

"Yes."

"Well, I'm glad I've put the fear of God in you."

"This is absurd. What do I have to be afraid of? I'm here because

I know something's wrong. It's not like Edwin not to be in touch. And you were asking about him. You were asking about the priest as well. That's not a coincidence."

"You're the one who brought the priest into it, not me."

"And now he's dead."

"So you *are* afraid."

"Stop that this minute. You pester me while I'm having lunch, you hurl accusations at me, there's something the matter with you."

"If you say so."

"I know who you are. You're an undertaker."

"Well done. You've done your homework. Blum Funerary Institute, we're a traditional firm. I can plan your funeral if you pay in advance. I'll be happy to see to it personally."

"You're going to tell me what you want from me, and what you know about the whereabouts of my son. Then you're going to tell me why you're muckraking through ancient history."

"It's not that ancient. And from where I'm standing, you're still in the muck."

"You'd better pray nothing has happened to my son."

"Praying won't help, believe me."

"If you have anything to do with his disappearance, you'll have me to answer to."

"Oh, and will you lock me in a cage too?"

"I'll wipe that grin right off your face."

"I didn't think it would be so easy."

"I won't let you out of my sight."

"Father and son. The huntsman and the photographer. And the village priest. What a trio. All we need now is the cook and the clown."

"As I said, I haven't the faintest idea what you're talking about, but I'm making it my business to find out."

"Be my guest."

"This isn't the last you'll hear from me."

He turned and walked away. She swallowed the retort that had been on the tip of her tongue. Schönborn's words went round and round in her head. He knew who she was, he had gone to the trouble of finding that out. Blum wanted to believe that Johannes Schönborn was the huntsman. It would be so simple, so obvious, father and son. While he was talking, she was picturing him on her preparation table; in her mind she was sawing off his arms and legs, taking him apart like the carcass of a deer. Briefly, she believed in his guilt. But now she realizes that he had nothing to do with it. Johannes Schönborn was not one of the men in the cellar. His face had given that away. In the restaurant and now here, his astonishment had been genuine, as had the confusion in his eyes. He really didn't have the faintest idea what she was talking about. No idea about the cages, the anesthetic darts, and the three names, which had meant nothing to him. Old Schönborn was just a worried man who wanted his son back. She decided he would live.

Blum is in the car on the way to the forensic laboratory. A body from the hospital is waiting for her; a woman in her midfifties, the autopsy was routine. She parks outside the gate, gets out, and waits for the lab assistant to bring her the body. She has been to this place so often. The refrigerators and the bodies stacked in the corridors are all so familiar to her. None of it bothers her, they are only unknown corpses in body bags, taken apart then stitched back together again. She has no emotional connection with these strangers; she is simply providing transport, moving a body from one fridge to the next.

Blum paces up and down the corridor. She thinks of how well the day began, of Jaunig's study, of the menu lying on his desk. She

179

hopes that her assumption is correct. It is the gut feeling that has been driving her since she left the apartment with Massimo. While she waits, she considers what to do next. Suddenly a familiar face is there beside Blum. Blum's eyes rest briefly on her, she almost didn't recognize her under the plastic film. Blum freezes. The rib cage is open and the skin is white. She has drowned. At first Blum can't get her thoughts in order or understand what she's seeing. She is lying in the cellar of the forensic laboratory, just like that, on a stretcher because there's no room for her in a fridge. Blum feels like screaming, but she can't, because it is suddenly cold, and quiet. Just another corpse, a nameless body that no one has missed. No one knows who she is.

For a long time there is nothing in her mind but Dunya. Blum is unable to react, there's only Dunya, all that happened, how they met. At first she was only a voice, then a face, then a smile. Blum stares at her. There was nothing she could say to help, nothing that could undo what had happened. Blum forces herself not to cry, to show no emotion. She doesn't want anyone to realize that she knew the woman, that there was a connection. The mortuary assistant draws Blum away from Dunya, annoyed that she is trans-fixed by this body. Then he asks whether she is all right, can he help her, would she like a glass of water?

The mortuary assistant answered all her questions. He didn't know why Blum wanted to know, but he told her all the same. *It was probably suicide, or an accident. The autopsy confirms that she drowned. There is nothing to suggest foul play. People were quite often found,* he said, *in the grid of the Inn power station. A dredger lifts them out of the water along with trash and trees. The grid is cleaned of flotsam every few weeks; she was found quite by chance.* One more drowned body, probably a homeless person, a woman without papers who doesn't match the missing persons records. *Very likely she was drunk and fell in. Or she was tired of life and jumped. One way or another, dead is dead,* the mortuary assistant said.

Blum is in the hearse with the woman in her midfifties, the victim of a coronary thrombosis resulting from a lung transplant; her family have already brought her clothes to the Funerary Institute. Blum is on her way home. She will carefully remove the woman from the body bag, wash her, clean her wounds, stitch her mouth closed, and dress her again. She yearns to do the same for Dunya, to tend to her violated body, to show her affection and respect. But Dunya must stay where she is; they will put her in the long-term storage room, where the temperature is lower. Corpses often stay there for months: the people who can't be identified, murder victims when investigations are ongoing. People like Jaunig. Dunya will probably share a refrigerator with his head. Perpetrator and victim stacked peacefully together. Fate is cruel, and Blum can't do anything about that. She feels as though she has taken a running jump into a pool emptied of water. She plunges in headfirst, without stopping to breathe. Blum drives through the city in the hearse, her tears falling quietly.

34

How many tears we have. If only we could count them, catch them, fill a beaker with them, a bucket. A swimming pool. Then it wouldn't hurt to dive in headfirst. Blum hasn't been able to breathe properly for three days. She does her work, she stays with the children, she tries to go on living. But the sadness is back and it's crippling. It is hard for Blum to accept that she was unable to help Dunya. She should have watched her more closely, she should have protected her. Blum has failed. If she hadn't let her go to the supermarket alone, she might still be alive. That idea hurts. From Moldavia to the cellar, from the cellar to the refrigerator.

Retreat or attack? Blum has been pondering the question for three days. Should she act as though everything might get better, or smash it all apart? Three days of time lost. But the rage within her rises again. She doesn't doubt for a moment that Dunya was murdered. She didn't jump, she didn't just fall into the water, and she didn't run away. She felt at ease in the girls' bedroom, she would have come back. Someone silenced her then disposed of her, threw her into the water like a dead fish. She saw Dunya's gaping mouth in the forensics lab, silent and cold.

Someone else has been murdered. First Ilena, then Mark, now Dunya. She thinks of nothing else for three days, she torments herself, she forces herself to think of another explanation for what has happened. She briefly considers forgetting the whole thing, deciding just to be happy with the children. But she can't. Mark isn't here, nor is their old life, and her new one is only just beginning to take shape. Blum drinks wine on her terrace. Her thoughts are all over the place, the children have gone to sleep on her lap. Whatever they say, whatever they do, they cannot make everything better. She thinks of what Nela said before she fell asleep.

"Mama?"

"Yes, darling?"

"I feel happy in my tummy."

"Happy?"

"Yes, I feel all happy."

"Why?"

"I saw Papa."

"You did what?"

"He's fine, Mama. He was on his motorcycle and he smiled at me. And he waved, Mama."

"No."

"Yes, Mama, and he said you mustn't be sad."

"Did he?"

"Yes, he did."

He has been dead for so long now. The last time they touched, the last time they shared a smile, feels so far in the past. Blum would have loved to see what Nela saw. She would have loved to spare her daughter everything. Because there are murderers out there, murderers who ruin everything. Blum drinks, and cuddles her children. It is a beautiful autumn night, the sky is clear, everything is simple. They have struck and now Blum is striking back because there's nothing else to be done, nothing that will bring Mark back to her. She will find the other men, but for now she will go to sleep with her children.

The next morning Karl takes over as usual. Reza asks Blum what her plans are. Blum says nothing but smiles at him, just as Mark smiled at Nela. *Don't worry about me, Reza. I'll be back. I can look after myself, you can count on that. Thank you, Reza.* Blum gets on the motorcycle, rides down the drive and out into the street on her way to Kitzbühel. She knows her plan will probably get her nowhere, but she carries it out all the same. It was a flash of inspiration. She saw that menu and wondered what it was doing there. A menu from a restaurant in Kitzbühel, lying on the desk of a priest in Innsbruck. Why would he have taken it with him? Why would a priest steal a menu? Or did the priest know the restaurateur so well he could take it with him? It's fifty-four kilometers to the restaurant in Kitzbühel, Puch's Place. She is going to act on her hunch.

On the outskirts of Kitzbühel, near the woods, the rich have conjured up so many buildings: vacation homes, second apartments, and this restaurant, which has been awarded Michelin stars. The restaurant is quite small, it seats forty. Blum asks about the chef. Everyone knows who she's looking for, everyone knows the cook off the television: Bertl Puch. It's an excellent restaurant, an unassuming exterior but obviously of high quality and very expensive. It is lunchtime, but the customers wear evening dresses and suits. Blum has always hated Kitzbühel, that mecca of the rich, that seat of money and power. These people stick together, stuffing themselves with weisswurst and caviar. They are among their own, apart from the common herd.

Blum is asked to leave; the waiter points out the dress code. But Blum stands her ground. She has nothing to lose, she wants to know whether she is on the right track; she intends to find out whether the chef and the photographer knew each other. And the chef and the priest. She undresses in full view of the room, removing her leather jacket, trousers, boots. She takes high heels out of her bag. The customers look at her long legs, her bare feet, and then she is transformed like a swan, standing there in a flowery summer dress. She stows her leathers away in her rucksack. The waiter stares at her, wide-eyed. Gritting his teeth, he agrees that she can stay, and shows her to a table. Blum sits down.

She feels ill at ease; she hates pretentious restaurants. But she is here for Dunya. She orders and tries to strike up a conversation with the waiter. He is very discreet and ignores Blum's questions about the owner. When will Bertl Puch be back? Did Herbert Jaunig come here often? She receives no answer during the starter or the next course. But then, suddenly, the woman at the next table joins her. She is exactly the sort of gossip Blum was hoping to meet. All sorts of information is served up with the third course. *My name is Kordula Heidmann*, says the woman. She is in her midfifties, clearly as rich as Croesus. Blum pricks up her ears and takes in the woman's remodeled face, her clothes, her designer handbag, a watch that must have cost a fortune. Everything about her stinks of money. She comes here quite often, she says, whispering that she can tell Blum more. And she does, with relish. Blum is the highlight of her day. She scrutinizes the exotic beauty in the flowery summer dress with curiosity. Kordula Heidmann holds forth without asking why Blum is taking such an interest in Bertl Puch. Blum glances at her plate: chocolate-coated duck breast on whole wheat bread. She cuts up her duck breast while Kordula Heidmann tells her all about Bertl Puch. And Herbert Jaunig.

"Unfortunately the chef isn't here."

"Where is he, do you know? I'd have liked to meet him so much. He's the talk of all the Tyrol."

"All the Tyrol? All Austria, you mean. He's such a talented man, everything he touches turns to gold. You've no idea how lucky we are to have him here."

"You are indeed."

"At the moment he's filming the new season of his cooking show in Vienna. He's a busy man, and still so young. What a wonderful example his career sets! You really have to take your hat off to him. People come from all over the country to enjoy his cuisine. The dishes are just spectacular, don't you agree?"

"Yes, spectacular, you're quite right."

"You should see what he can do with quail eggs. And the lamb, you've never eaten such tender lamb."

"May I ask you something?"

"Of course, go ahead!"

"Father Jaunig—Herbert Jaunig. Did you know him?"

"Oh, yes. What a tragedy. And such a delightful man. He loved food, he was a real gourmet. All the regulars here were horrified by the news. You can't imagine how terrible I felt when I heard it."

"You were a friend of his?"

"Oh, no, but I often sat close to him, watching him."

"Watching him do what?"

"Eating lunch or dinner. He was a good man, Father Jaunig."

"Indeed he was."

"He used to sit over there, always the same table. It was a pleasure to see him enjoying a meal."

"Did he come on his own?"

"Usually. I once tried to sit with him, but he was deep in prayer. He said he took every opportunity to pray for us. What a fine man. Beheaded! I still can't believe it."

"It does sound bizarre."

"Who would do a thing like that? Only a monster, an animal."

"Suppose Father Jaunig deserved it?"

"For God's sake, what makes you say a thing like that? Never! No one deserves to die that way. What could that good man have done to justify such a dreadful murder? I'll tell you something, there's a sick mind behind all this."

"You're probably right."

"Of course I'm right."

"And what about Herr Puch?"

"How do you mean, what about him?"

"Well, he and Jaunig knew each other."

"Knew each other? Those two were bosom buddies. Inseparable! It was a really wonderful relationship between two men."

"Friendships like that are rare."

"This whole business has upset Bertl dreadfully. He's devastated."

"I suppose they'd known each other for a long time, had they?"

"I think they met in the Ötztal."

"The Ötztal?"

"Yes, Bertl was a chef there before he opened this restaurant. At the Hotel Annenhof, a simple little place. Good plain cooking, hardly Michelin-starred. And suddenly his career took off. Bertl became a superstar in just five years."

"Wow!"

"There isn't a better restaurant in Kitzbühel."

"From a provincial hotel to gourmet heaven. I expect you know all the regulars here, don't you?"

"Well, not every single one, but as I said, anyone who's anyone comes here. The top people, if you see what I mean, from the president of Austria to Arnold Schwarzenegger. They all eat here."

"Does the name Edwin Schönborn mean anything to you?"

"The photographer—of course. He's also a regular."

"And another friend of Bertl?"

"Bertl knows everyone. And everyone wants to be his friend. You know how it is. Wine tastes best in famous company."

"Well, here's to your very good health."

Blum wipes her mouth. She thinks of her children's Lego pieces, brick on top of brick. Whenever she reaches for one it fits. Schönborn. Jaunig. Puch. Dunya did everything she could. She told Mark and Blum what mattered. Dunya didn't know their names or faces but Blum has managed to track them down. Two of them, and soon she'll have the third.

Dunya told her what the cook did to them, how he fattened them up. *I have to feed my little piggies well*, he always said. Only the best was put through the openings in the cages, good food, good meat, only the best for the pigs he was fattening. Dunya had told her how he inspected them, weighed them, made them get undressed every time he went down to the cellar. *It's important to check on their health*, he would say. He weighed them and kept records. And he made sure they did exercises to stay fit. *But good food is the most important thing, it's no fun fucking a starving deer*, he would add, hitting them with his belt when they wouldn't eat any more. They ate tournedos with goose liver pâté from plastic bowls, their hands tied behind their backs. They stuffed themselves with coquilles St. Jacques in champagne sauce. They were kept like animals and slept on hay, often pissing themselves because they couldn't get to the toilet in time. Gourmet cooking and the smell of piss. *Pearls before swine*, said the clown. All the same, the cook insisted on a balanced diet. *We must feed our little piggies well*, he said. *We must muck out the filthy swine*, said the clown. And the priest washed them with a garden hose, the water hitting them full force on their faces and on their wounds. They had to strip naked. They had to clean out their cages, scrub the floor. They had to do everything they were told, for years on end. With sweetbreads and escargot.

Blum pays her bill and leaves. She wants to get out of this place, she doesn't want to hear any more or replay the scenes from that cellar. At first she couldn't believe that people were kept in cages, waiting to be fed. She must find Youn, she can't let another person die. *Not one of the good ones, no, please no.* Someone must talk.

Blum is on her motorcycle again, riding fast along the highway back to her life, back to the villa and her little world, which is intact even though Mark is dead. It is intact because she is free, because she can do whatever she wants. No one is stopping her, no one will dissuade her from cutting up Bertl Puch. She wants to know what he is like. She wants to fill in the blanks and get to know this man who casts a spell over everyone he meets. Who beat the three people in the cellar with his belt, masturbating as he did so. Bertl Puch is on her TV screen, on YouTube, that busy little chef with the broad grin and the Tyrolean dialect who has risen to stratospheric heights. The nation's darling, the man with the beaming smile who makes every housewife think she can change the world with a spoon. She will track him down and find out whether he really is as she imagines him. Blum will talk to him and then she will kill him. Soon.

35

There, on the second floor of a building on Neubaugasse, in Vienna's District Seven, is a small apartment looking onto the street. The lock is no problem; Mark showed her what to do years ago. They had locked themselves out, but he managed to open the door in a couple of minutes. *It's child's play,* he said. Bertl Puch is on his way to the TV station and will be busy all day. Studio One has been booked for the week to film his cooking show. Blum waited outside the TV station for him yesterday, followed him, sat in the same bar as he did, drinking a beer, and observed him at play. He was a popular man, and looked just as innocent as his friends. None of them would believe what she knew. When he paid and left, Blum followed him. She sat in the same U-Bahn car. He traveled six stops, then another ten minutes on foot. He opened the front door of his building and disappeared inside. A light went on. From the street, Blum saw his silhouette in a second-floor window. Bertl Puch was at home in his Viennese apartment, the star chef was about to go to bed. Twenty minutes later the light went off. Blum stayed where she was a little longer, then went to collect her car. She waited until a parking spot was free with a good view of the front door, then lay down in the back of the car and set her alarm. She slept until five in the morning and then moved to the front seat. She waited until he left the building. Bertl Puch was on his way to work.

An elderly woman let herself into the building. Blum walked in behind her, as though it were the most natural thing in the world. She smiled at the old lady, who smiled back before going through a door on the ground floor. There was no nameplate on the door, just a lock. A screwdriver, a piece of wood, and a hammer were all it took. Only a faint knocking sound could be heard, and then the door opens and closes behind her. Blum is in his apartment with plastic covers over her shoes, a plastic hood on her head, and gloves. Mark always used to tell her how stupid criminals were, how many clues they left at the scene of the crime: hair, sweat, skin, fingerprints. Blum will do everything by the book. Nothing she leaves in the apartment must betray a search, for evidence, for videos.

The laptop isn't password protected. It is on the coffee table, flanked by potato chips and two empty beer cans. Everything is untidy, there are smears of grease on the computer screen. Blum turns it on. How stupid he is, how very careless. In spite of the chaos of his apartment, Bertl Puch's computer is tidy, the files are neatly arranged. Blum spots what she is looking for at once, the letters cry out to her. Pig-breeding, they say. Pig-breeding.

Blum in someone else's apartment, doing things that would have been unimaginable a couple of months ago. She doesn't stop to think. She'll do whatever it takes to find out whether this man really was connected to Mark's death, to Dunya's death. Blum crossed a line when she handed Schönborn the bottle, when she put him in those caskets. The line has been crossed, the border is open, there is no barbed wire there now. Blum has burnt Jaunig to death and cut his head off. She thought of Dunya as she did it. She saw those empty eyes in Edwin Schönborn's photographs. They were monsters: Schönborn and Jaunig and Puch, the chef.

He had filmed the pig-breeding videos on his cell, then saved them to his laptop. Anyone could have found them, could have watched what went on in that cellar. There was no attempt at conceal-ment; it hadn't occurred to Bertl Puch that someone might steal his laptop and investigate his pig-breeding. He feels safe. He sees no reason to delete those seventeen horror films. They document feeding time, training sessions, and punishments. They feature Dunya, Ilena, and Youn. Dunya was as Blum knew her, but more ravaged, more wounded. She was in the middle of hell and could see no way out. Their faces were devoid of despair, betraying only resignation, a silent cry for release. Silent because they had no strength left, nothing but the wish to die. Dunya said they had longed for death, thought of release all the time, but couldn't think how to kill themselves. So they had borne the violence and humil-iations. Blum endured these brief glimpses into a sick, sick world. The room had been specially prepared. The cages were tiled so the captives could be washed. The dirty zone, the fucking zone, were kept strictly separate. The videos showed feeding time, the kicks and blows they endured while they ate, the lust and rage, the pun-ishment. It was the cook's project and it amused him. He recorded a voice-over while he filmed the ungrateful little pigs who despised the delicacies from his famous little restaurant. She sees Bertl Puch beating them until they bleed, his belt in one hand, his cell in the other. Punishment was meted out in the dirty zone. Pregnant Ilena lay on the floor, no longer moving. Youn had to eat everything out of the buckets, every last scrap.

Blum sits in Bertl Puch's apartment and clicks through the videos. In some of them you can see the priest hosing Youn down, wash-ing and tending to him before assaulting him again. She recognizes his stature, his voice. And Schönborn is there too, holding his camera. Blum is 100 percent sure that's him, in spite of the mask. She has seen him naked, seen his disassembled parts, she knows it's him. The cellar is a land outside the law, an orgy where everything is allowed and nothing is forbidden. Not even the anesthetizing darts fired from the hunting rifle. The videos show exactly what Dunya described. She was right, there was nowhere to run.

She doesn't recognize the fourth man. He wears a larger mask than the others and has an ordinary body. The only thing Blum can say for certain is that he isn't Schönborn's father. Johannes Schönborn is stronger and weighs about twenty kilos more than the man in the video. He shrieks with glee as he presses the trigger, he yodels, he sings. What Blum sees disturbs her. It is the performance of a madman. A half-naked man doing a victory dance round the fucking area, which is padded and plush velvet. The huntsman is happy to be shooting, he exudes joie de vivre. At the top of his voice, he sings one of the best-known songs in the world, "O sole mio." *There is no lovelier sun*. Youn lies on the floor. The huntsman bawls out the song. *Ma n'atu sole cchiù bello, oi né*. He sings ardently, with passion, almost well. If Blum had heard only his voice, she would have liked him. *O sole mio*, while he rapes Youn.

The huntsman is singing to the camera. He poses, it is a private performance for the cook. This little video is telling Blum everything she needs to know because his face is shown, just for a moment. She hadn't expected him to reveal the mystery himself, to remove his mask for two seconds, just as the video is coming to an end. She makes out his eyes, his nose; he is grinning into the camera, basking in the scene. After two seconds, he puts the mask back on. In those two seconds, she sees the rapist, the murderer, the evidence of his guilt. Blum rewinds the tape, watches it again and again, then presses Stop.

She has seen that face before. She is 100 percent sure that she knows him but she has no idea where from. A name goes with that face. He is an actor, the hero of a television series. Blum has seen him while channel surfing. Something about the wonderful world of the mountains, beautiful landscapes, and love. No one would ever have thought he led a double life. He is the huntsman.

Blum rejoices. She was expecting to have to turn the apartment upside down. She was expecting to spend the whole day here, rummaging. But after an hour she is back out on the street. She has found what she was looking for. She has transferred the videos to a USB stick and deleted the originals from his hard disk. She has left no trace. No one will guess the reason for what is going to happen next. Bertl Puch will disappear into thin air, just like that. He won't be going back to the studio, he won't be filming any more shows, he'll never go back to Kitzbühel, never cook for Kordula Heidmann again. Blum passed sentence the minute she pressed Play. She will take the chef out of circulation. The huntsman too. And quickly.

In Vienna, no one stops her, no one persuades her not to do it, no one tells her to abandon her plan, tells her not to phone and meet Puch, not to kill him, not to anesthetize him, stab him, chop off his head with an ax. She feels intoxicated as she lays plans to get him into her car unseen, take him to Innsbruck, and snuff him out like a candle. Press the switch and off goes the light. The light will go out and he will be just another body on her table, skin and fat as she draws her needle through his flesh.

36

"Bertl Puch here."

"Listen carefully."

"Who is this?"

"If you don't want your story to be on television, then listen hard. I know everything. I know about the cellar, about your pig-breeding, about Schönborn and the actor. I know what you and the others did, I know you killed the police officer. And the girl as well. There's evidence, and it is deposited with a notary. If he doesn't hear from me he is going to hand over the files to the press. Do you understand?"

"Yes."

"Now, do exactly as I say. Go to the end of the street. There's an underground garage on the right. Go down to the second floor, bay two hundred and four. Wait for me there."

"Where are you?"

"Right behind you."

"Where?"

"Get moving."

"What the hell do you want?"

"I repeat, if you don't do as I say, I'll make your life a living hell."

"What do you want from me? Where did you get this phone number? How the fuck do I know that you breed pigs?"

"Turn round and continue. Bay two hundred and four. When I park, you will open the trunk and get into the casket."

"Do what?"

"You heard me."

"Are you insane?"

"The choice is yours: either you get into that casket or in an hour's time the world will be watching your delightful home videos."

"You've been in my apartment?"

"And your restaurant."

"I want to know what you're after."

"I don't care what you want."

"You're behind me . . . That's a hearse you're driving, isn't it? Are you out of your mind?"

"It's a Cadillac Superior, built in 1972. You'll have a very comfortable ride."

"Leave me alone."

"I can stay here or I can drive away. The decision is yours."

"Who are you? What's all this shit about? This can't be happening."

"If you don't go into the garage right now, I am leaving."

"You want me to get into a casket?"

"That's right. Bay two hundred and four. You will put your phone on the roof of the car and open the trunk. If you try opening the driver's door or attacking me your life is over. So just get into the casket and lie down. I'll get out and close the lid."

"Are you out of your fucking mind?"

"If you don't follow my instructions, you're finished."

In bay 204, Blum switches the engine off. There are no CCTV cameras trained on this bay. It's a blind spot. The ideal place to invite the pig breeder and seal his fate. Bertl Puch now stands behind the car looking doubtful. Blum can hear him breathing into his phone. The disgusting, oyster-slurping bastard is trying to think of a way out. For ten seconds nothing happens, there's only the sound of his breathing. Bertl Puch is standing behind the car, wondering whether to run or attack. Blum can see and hear his desperation and fury. She doesn't want her plan to fail, she doesn't want him to run for it, so she decides not to wait a second longer. Blum turns the key and puts the car into reverse. *You asked for it*, she says, disconnecting the call.

The cook leaps aside, then tries to stop her. He doesn't want her to drive away. He bangs on the windows with the palm of his hand. When he shouts *stay*, Blum engages the brake. She turns her head to look at him, a smile playing on her lips. *Don't be afraid. Just climb in. Trust me*. It is a gracious smile, and he puts his phone on the roof of the car and raises his hands in the air. *I'll do what you want for now*, those hands say. *I want to know what happens next, what you're planning. I want another chance. I'll get an opportunity to kill you. That's why I'm getting into your fucking casket, you sick slut*. That's what his raised hands say, and his eyes and the twist of his mouth. She sees him stare through the window, put his phone on the roof of the Cadillac, and open the trunk. Like a lamb to the slaughter, Bertl Puch lies down in the casket. Blum puts her forefinger to her lips just before she closes the lid. *Not a word*, she says as she screws it into place. There is no way he could get out of the casket unaided. It is Blum's best model, a massive walnut-wood box, a thing of beauty with a 2,500-euro price tag.

Blum drives away, leaving nothing behind. Bertl Puch has disappeared, and no one but Blum will ever set eyes on him again. They'll look for him, they'll go through his apartment with a fine-tooth comb, but they won't find him. No one has any idea that she knows him, no one will suspect Blum because no one knows the truth. No one knows the truth because no one wants to know that the death of the woman in the forensics lab wasn't accidental. Only Blum knows what happened, she and the cook, the actor, and the clown. Blum is on her own. There is no police squad to back her up, so she gave her words emphasis, she had seen this kind of thing on television, she has read it in books. My life insurance is in a safe-deposit box. A marksman has you in his sights. It worked so well. She has intimidated him with what she knows. The reality scared him and he has cut off every escape route. Bertl Puch got into a casket of his own free will. Bertl Puch is going to die.

37

It is afternoon and they are on the highway just outside Linz. For over an hour, he has been hammering on the lid of the casket with his fists. Blum listens to music; Freddie Mercury competes with the screams of Bertl Puch. "The Show Must Go On." After a while, the TV chef realizes that nothing he can do will make the car stop, that his shouting is pointless. By Sankt Pölten only Freddie can be heard and Blum drives fast. She passes Linz. It's only a hearse speeding along the highway, three and a half hours away from the Tyrol. Three and a half hours breathing in the stench of urine coming from the casket. Enough time to remember Hagen and that woman.

Blum was ten years old. Hagen made her watch an old lady being prepared for her funeral. It was high summer and hot, and Blum was much too young. Hagen wouldn't stop tormenting her. *Brünhilde, you stay here. You're going to watch what I do now. This is your vocation, Brünhilde. But I'm a child*, she had pleaded. He began cutting the old woman's clothes from her body. She was grossly fat, the most horrible thing Blum had ever seen. Hagen wouldn't let her leave the room, and so Blum cried. It had taken four people to haul the old woman out of the car and lower her by crane onto the preparation table. She was huge; an oversize mountain of flesh, her skin struggling to contain her fat. Blum was disgusted and wanted to run away from the smell. But Hagen took hold of Blum's arm and held it firmly. *Stay here, Brünhilde. Now you are going to learn how we deal with excrement.* Blum stayed, and Hagen showed her what to do when a corpse's intestines are still full.

The smell of urine overwhelms Blum. The old woman had wet herself. Her skin stank, everything about her stank of piss and shit. It came flowing out of her anus, refusing to stop, the tampon Hagen had tried inserting was no match for the torrent. There was shit everywhere, on his white gloves, on the preparation table, on the old woman's thighs. Hagen's assistants held her legs up, while Hagen stitched the anus up. *This is the only thing to do in a situation like this, Brünhilde. There's no alternative. We have to stitch up her anus, Brünhilde.* Shit, brown, stinking shit, kept flowing from the fat woman's body. Blum wasn't there to help, only to watch, and that made it even worse. On other days, when she had to lend a hand, she didn't have time to think or feel revulsion. She had to concentrate on pushing the needle through skin and fat. Watching was worse, much worse. She remembers Hagen's brown fingers swiftly stitching the anus of that fat, dead woman who had covered everything in shit. Those are the images that return every time she smells piss and shit.

Just after Sankt Pölten, Bertl Puch lost control of his bowels in the walnut casket. Now she can smell his fear. Almost twenty-two years ago, Blum wanted to run away from that smell. It all began with that smell, and now it seems it's going to end with that smell. Deep down, Blum knows she can't go on like this. It's as though her guardian angel has gone off duty. Heaven has turned again, and Blum is swaying. Last time everything came together seamlessly; this time everything is coming apart. Just before Salzburg she has to brake. She's driving too fast. A policeman has been following her and makes her leave the highway and drive to a rest stop. A young man dressed in plain clothes gestures for her to open her window, and instead of rolling it down, Blum turns the music up and gets out. It's her only option. She quickly slams the car door behind her, trusting that the music inside will drown out the noise Puch is making. Because he has begun to shout again and kick the walls of the wooden box. She hopes Puch won't be heard. Blum tries to smile and ignore the fact that the officer is an asshole.

"Your driver's license and registration."

"I guess I was over the speed limit?"

"Ah, so you know you were driving too fast? That makes it a premeditated offense. You ignored the speed limit and thus deliberately endangered the lives of other motorists."

"I'm terribly sorry. My mind drifted."

"Had it now? Is that because you've been drinking?"

"No . . . I just didn't notice the speed limit. I was deep in thought."

"This will cost you a pretty penny. Your driver's license will be ready for collection in Salzburg in a month's time."

"No . . . I mean, I can't . . ."

"I decide what you can and can't do. You were almost fifty kph over the limit."

"I know, it's unforgivable."

"This isn't a question of forgiveness. You'll have to call a vehicle to tow you the rest of your journey."

"Oh, please no—you can see what I'm transporting."

"This is a hearse, right?"

"Yes, the Blum Funerary Institute, Innsbruck."

"A white hearse?"

"Yes, my father really wanted it."

"So your father is the undertaker?"

"I'm sorry to say my father is dead. Now I run the business."

"But you're a woman."

"And?"

"That's no job for a woman."

"If you say so."

"Why is the music so loud?"

"As a woman, I find it distressing to drive corpses around. The music helps."

"Don't you think that's disrespectful to the dead?"

"That hadn't occurred to me but I'll give it some thought."

"You should."

"Can't you turn a blind eye? Leave me my driver's license? I'll happily pay the fine, but I really must get this corpse to Innsbruck. The family is expecting it."

"Who's in the box?"

"An old lady. She's been in the water a long time."

"A drowned body?"

"That's right."

"I've never seen one of those."

"You're not missing out, believe me."

"I'd like to see a drowned body. May I take a peek inside?"

"I don't think that's a good idea."

"I'm used to all sorts of things, mark my word. Just the other day we picked up a body from the railway tracks. The head was mush. And there was that accident on the Attersee four days ago. Seven dead."

"What a difficult job you do."

"It doesn't bother me. So show me what's inside the box."

"You can't be serious."

"Of course I'm serious. How often do I get a chance to see a drowned body? This must be my lucky day."

"It's really not a good idea."

"Come now—you show me the body and we'll forget your little misdemeanor."

"But it stinks. And there are little bits of skin everywhere, and that face. That face!"

"Doesn't bother me. Come on, let's have a look."

"Please understand. As a woman it isn't easy for me to look at these things. I actually threw up when I loaded it in. I just want to get the body properly buried."

"An undertaker who's afraid of bodies?"

"Please. Don't do this to me."

"Women. I've always said they should stay in the kitchen."

"Yes, right."

"I can make you open up, you know."

"Please don't. Not today."

"Then when?"

"Well, I have photos."

"What sort of photos?"

"Pictures of bodies. Lots and lots of bodies. Beheadings, hanged bodies, bodies that got crushed, corpses after autopsies, amputees. Everything, believe me. I have thousands of photos and you can study them at your leisure. Come to Innsbruck and I'll show you things you've never seen before."

"That sounds good. That sounds very good indeed. And you definitely have pictures of drowning victims?"

"Several, yes. We keep records of everything. And the best thing is that pictures don't stink."

"I'll come and see you in Innsbruck."

"The Blum Funerary Institute. You're welcome to drop by anytime."

"Let's forget about the fine, why don't we?"

"Thank you."

"Drive carefully."

"I will."

"And think about what I said."

"What?"

"About staying in the kitchen."

Blum stands, fixed to the spot, as the grinning psychopath gets into his car and drives away. She is burning with terror. He almost opened the trunk, he already had his finger on the button. One second more and he would have heard the cries for help. She'd have lost everything: her life, her children. The idea of leaving them alone is the worst thing of all and it had very nearly come to that. Deep down, Blum is screaming. Her life almost slipped away from her grasp and she has no one else to blame but herself: she had abducted a man in broad daylight without knocking him out. She had been driving too fast, she had turned up the music too loud. She hates herself and longs to be back in control. She mustn't take any more risks. And that is why she needs to do it, this instant. She must silence him.

She hits him five times in close succession, allowing herself no time to calm down. She is out of control now, she is hitting him on the head with the jack, striking with all her might. She hits him before he realizes what is going on. Then she hits him a second time and a third time. She feels no pity as she swings her arm back and hits him a fourth time, as hard as she can. There is a dull crunch, metal on skin and bone. A fifth time. His head is covered with blood; the smell is horrible. Blum quickly lowers the lid of the casket and screws it shut. Bertl Puch has stopped screaming. For a moment, calm descends. She closes the trunk and turns around. She is in a small rest stop just off the highway. Her heart is racing as she stares straight ahead. She is not alone.

38

You can see it all from above. The parking place, the hearse, a woman on the ground beside it. She is lying facedown on the asphalt, she doesn't move. Her mouth is open, the sun is shining. She doesn't move, she can't, she doesn't want to, it simply won't work. Her eyes are open but they can't settle, her vision is dissolving. Her body is doubled up. She can't move an inch, she just lies where she is. She lies by the highway like a child feeling cold, waiting for an adult to bring her a blanket. Blum is helpless and alone.

Down and down she goes into the abyss. All of a sudden he was there. Blum hadn't seen him arrive but he had seen it all. He saw her silencing Bertl Puch, then he jumped into his car and sped away. There was no chance to react; there was nothing more she could do. Fate had kicked her in the guts. The fact that a man saw her killing Bertl Puch hits her. She has killed a man, violently, without hesitation, and she was observed.

Was the driver just stopping for a rest, answering a call of nature, or did he know what was going to happen all along? Now he has driven away, leaving her alone but for a bloodied Bertl Puch and a terrible sense of helplessness in the pit of her stomach. Blum doesn't know her right hand from her left, doesn't know what to do, what would be good for her and what wouldn't. Her mind is spinning out of control. And then there's the pain which forces her to her knees like a blow. Her vehicle is conspicuous; in a couple of hours, the police could be at her door. Uma and Nela would scream as she got into the patrol car. She pictures their faces, the questions in their eyes, their flailing arms trying to help her, to halt her departure. Blum sees what is going to happen. The real world is dissolving and scenes of horror are swimming before her eyes.

Blum is trembling. She remembers the mess that was Bertl Puch, his pulpy head, his blood, his shit, his urine. She must get up, she must drive away from here. She must limit the damage, turn back the clock as best she can, dispose of him in a grave. She must go to the children, hold them in her arms, tell them she loves them, kiss them, laugh with them, act as if everything is all right. At least one last time. She must hope that nothing will separate them. She'd give everything for that, do anything for it, tell lies, deny accusations, kill for it too. Blum will stand up now and get into her car. She will ignore the smell, drive back to Innsbruck, and take refuge in the preparation room. Bertl Puch will disappear. She will clean the casket and reset her life.

She emerges from her fainting fit and gets back into the hearse. She drives away from the rest stop and onto the highway, from Salzburg on to Innsbruck. Blum is hanging from strings but she is the puppet master. She forces herself to get up, raises her arm, puts her hand on the steering wheel, presses her foot on the accelerator. Then she taps a number into her phone.

"Where are you? What's the matter?"
"I just wanted to hear your voice, Massimo."
"Are you driving?"

"It doesn't matter."

"What's the matter, Blum?"

"Suppose something happens to me. What would happen to the children?"

"What would happen to you?"

"I might die."

"What the hell are you talking about?"

"Mark's dead. I might die too, and then the children would be on their own."

"You mustn't think like that."

"But I do. And it frightens me."

"Well, stop."

"They'll be put into a home."

"Stop talking like that. Nothing's going to happen to you, I'll look after you. Trust me."

"Do you remember the woman Mark was meeting?"

"Yes. Why?"

"She's dead."

"What are you talking about?"

"They pulled her out of the River Inn. I saw her in the forensics lab."

"How do you know it was her? You don't know the woman."

"I saw a photo on Mark's cell. I know what she looked like. And she's dead, Massimo. Drowned. They say it was either accident or suicide."

"Oh, Blum, you mustn't let this weigh on your mind. It's got nothing to do with you."

"It had something to do with Mark."

"But Mark is dead. You must stop this, Blum. The woman was homeless. She probably got drunk and fell into the river. Or she was tired of life and just wanted to end it all."

"I'm frightened, Massimo."

"Please don't worry, Blum. I'll look into the case, I promise. I'll find out how she died. But you must promise you'll stop thinking the worst."

"I promise."

"It will get better, Blum."

"It's getting worse."

"Can I come and see you when the children go to bed?"

"Yes."

Blum ends the call. The thought of lying in his arms does make it better. The thought of telling him the truth is tempting. She would like to surrender herself, let him take control. Sure as she is that Massimo will never be more than a friend, she wishes he could be, wishes he could be like Mark to her. She wants to tell him everything about Dunya, Schönborn, Jaunig, and Puch. She doesn't want to be alone with it anymore, lying in a rest stop. Massimo will come when the children are asleep. Or perhaps he will come sooner, if someone called the police, saying he saw Blum hit a man with a jack.

39

A child's bike is under the apple tree. Nela is blowing bubbles. They float past Uma, who is asleep in her stroller. And here is Blum, parking the hearse behind the house and pushing the casket into the preparation room. It is late summer and the scene in the yard is so ordinary. Karl is pruning the black currant bushes, and Blum lifts Uma out of her stroller and kisses her awake. They run round the house, playing catch. Blum tries to forget the chef, to put off the inevitable. She'll give herself two hours, then she'll go back to the casket, to the body of Bertl Puch.

What follows is routine, and that helps. It is easier to touch a corpse than to watch someone else do it. Blum swathes herself in plastic: her hands, her arms, her legs, her shoes. She doesn't want to touch his blood or his flesh, she doesn't want to touch any part of him. Blum prepares the aspirator, saw, plastic bags, and formalin. She calculates she will have him apart in three hours; she'd like to dispose of him more quickly than she did Schönborn. She wants to go back to the yard, play catch with the children and pretend everything is okay. Blum lifts him with the crane and lowers him onto the preparation table. She cuts off the chef's clothes, undresses him, rolls him onto his side, and pulls the fabric away. She throws it all in the bin. His naked body looks innocent, his skin gives nothing away.

There is nothing to show that he is a murderer and a rapist. He could have been a respectable husband and father. If Blum hadn't known better, if she hadn't seen the videos and talked to him, she would think he was blameless and regret what she had done. But she knows she was right. She is doing what had to be done.

She turns up the music. She sprays disinfectant to cover up the smell of shit. She opens his rib cage and takes out his organs, just as she did with Schönborn. She creates as little mess as she can, channeling the blood down the drain and not letting it lie on the floor. She divides and packs up his organs, just as the butcher would do when Hagen bought game. Then Herta would divide the meat into portions and freeze it. Roe deer, red deer, sometimes a calf too, a pig. Blum saws off Bertl Puch's arms, then his legs. He is only flesh and bone. His limbs drop around her; she lets them fall to the floor and goes on sawing. She divides up his torso and separates his head from his neck. Just as his head drops off the table, the door opens.

The music was too loud. She didn't hear him coming, she'd forgotten to bolt the door. No one should have seen this; no one should have witnessed the crime. Blum has made her next mistake; she has lost control again. She can't forgive herself. Suppose it had been Nela standing in the doorway? Blum hadn't been paying attention and now he is staring at her. It is a bloodbath, a disaster, a crime. Bertl Puch's arms and legs and head are scattered on the floor. Blum would like the ground to swallow her up, she has no words, she just stands there, looking at him. Reza is taking in the scene, his eyes are circling the room, trying to make sense of it. Stepping forward, he closes the door and turns the key in the lock. Then he wraps himself in plastic without uttering a word. He dons an apron and a pair of gloves. Reza is getting ready for work. He ignores the obvious fact that Blum would like to shut him out, he just carries on where she left off. He takes the saw out of her hand and finishes carving Bertl Puch's torso.

"What are you doing, Reza?"

"Shouldn't I be asking you that question?"

"Go on, then, ask."

"No."

"It's complicated, Reza."

"It looks complicated. But we'll get it done. You were going to pack these things up, weren't you?"

"Yes."

"And then bury them?"

"Yes."

"We'll have to put some of them in storage. There's only one casket here, it won't all fit."

"No."

"Do you understand what I mean, Blum?"

"Yes."

"Last time the caskets were too heavy."

"What?"

"You overloaded them. The bearers noticed. I told them we were using a new model. A bigger casket, more wood."

"You knew?"

"I didn't know."

"Did you open the caskets?"

"No, I told you, they were too heavy."

"But you didn't say a thing?"

"No."

"It's all messed up. Something's . . . gotten out of control."

"You don't have to explain yourself to me."

"I think I do."

"I'm sure you had your reasons."

213

"I did."

"Well, that's good enough for me."

"Reza, leave and forget everything you've seen."

"No, we have to clean up now."

"I can explain it all."

"You don't have to."

"Mark's death. It wasn't an accident."

"What do you mean?"

"They killed him, Reza."

"Who did?"

"This man. And four others. They ran him over, they took him away from us. They blew out the candle on the cake, just like that."

Reza says nothing. He takes Bertl Puch's right arm, puts it into a plastic bag, pours in some formalin, and wraps it tightly. He fastens the little package with sticky tape. Bertl Puch's arm is almost vacuum-packed. Reza packs up his body piece by piece while Blum starts at the very beginning. With the recorded conversations, with Dunya in the supermarket, Schönborn in the forest, Jaunig on the boat, Dunya in the forensics lab, the actor singing on the video, the man in the rest stop. She tells him the horror story, the nightmare from which she can't awake. Now Reza is diving into the empty pool, hand in hand with her, to a count of three. She had no alternative. *I'm here for you*, he says, without pausing to think. There is no emotion on his face as he calmly wraps up the chef's head. He is not afraid. He just gets on with it. He raises his hand, then hurls the head into the corner to join the other packed-and-sealed parts of Bertl Puch.

"We'll get through this, Blum."

"I'm so sorry, Reza. I really didn't want to involve you in all this."

"Never mind that, Blum. I'm here."

"I've killed three people."

"I've killed ten."

"You don't judge me?"

"No, Blum. We'll get this one underground, then we'll see about that actor."

"We?"

"Yes, you and I."

"Thank you, Reza. You're wonderful."

"Don't say that."

"But, Reza, I feel so much better now I've told you. And it's great that you want to help me, although you're crazy to want to. If I were you, I'd run a million miles."

"I'd never let anything happen to you."

"But what about the man in the rest stop? He must have called the police."

"Everything's going to be okay."

Reza says so. He is standing in front of her. He removes his gloves, touching her face affectionately. The sensation of his palms on her cheeks is almost imperceptible. Reza gives her courage, he tries to rouse her from her nightmare. He tells her that life will go on, that Uma and Nela won't lose their mother, they are going to get through this. The remainder of Puch's dismembered torso is still on the table. She feels Reza's sudden closeness. The chef has come apart, and Reza's help does her good. They stand still and look at each other. Two murderers, with not a word to waste.

40

For a few hours, everything is okay. Blum entertains the hope that they have weathered the worst of the storm. She and Reza sit on Blum's sofa in the living room, having finished dinner and opened a bottle of wine. The children are asleep. Karl is finishing off in the garden. A gentle sense of security has crept back into her mind. It makes her cling to Reza; she doesn't want to let him go. After a while Reza puts his head back and closes his eyes. He is still awake when Blum nestles close to him, as her head comes to rest on his chest, as her hand gently holds his. He is a friend and he is there for her, he catches her, he plucks her out of the air and stops her thudding onto the bottom of the empty pool. His hands don't wander, he simply receives her. And she is grateful. Reza's chest rises and falls. Blum just lies there, sensing his presence, and it feels good. She wants to stay awake. She feels the link between them, the proximity, his restraint. Everything is both familiar and strange. She has known him for years as a faithful soul, a colleague, a friend. It would never have entered her head to touch him, to lie in his arms. Reza is shy, like a wild creature hiding in the forest, sparing with his words. He is like a shadow, a shadow in which she hides.

Outside she hears Karl mowing the lawn. It is getting dark, and there is nothing more to be done. For the moment there is only

Blum and Reza. But now Massimo is quietly coming upstairs, so quietly that she can barely hear him. Karl must have let him into the house. Blum has entirely forgotten that he was going to come, was offering her a shoulder to cry on. She hears his footsteps, closes her eyes, and pretends to be asleep. Her eyelids are open just a tiny crack. She sees him standing in the doorway, staring at the sofa, wondering what to do, what to say, whether to wake them. Massimo's eyes are wide. His face wears the expression of a beaten dog. Blum can see his disappointment, the pain she is inflicting by lying in another man's arms. Massimo stares. He sees two people sleeping; he doesn't know that Blum is awake and ashamed. He doesn't know that she feels sorry for him and would have liked to have spared him this.

Massimo stares at them for a long time. He has a bottle of wine in his left hand. He was going to drink it with Blum, he is here to console her, not to arrest her or question her. He doesn't know what happened in the rest stop. Whoever saw her hasn't gone to the police, or the uniformed men would have been here long ago to take her away. They'd have arrested her in the preparation room. There would have been no bottle in Massimo's hand.

He watches them sleep for a couple of minutes, and then he goes away without making a sound. As he steals downstairs and disappears, Blum opens her eyes. She wishes she had spared him. She hears the door close, and Karl turns off the lawn mower to ask why he's leaving so soon. Blum will explain, she will tell him that she was tired and lonely, it didn't mean a thing. But Massimo won't believe her, he will maintain he saw Blum and Reza's intimacy with his own eyes. He saw her head on his chest and her hand in his. Blum lies where she is, she doesn't want to get to her feet and run after him, she wants to stay with Reza.

That night she sleeps fitfully, plagued by bad dreams. Every time she wakes she is glad that he is still there, holding her. She keeps moving away, turning over, moving back towards him, and falling back asleep. Then a time comes when she opens her eyes and the day has begun. Uma is standing there, smiling and saying, *Mama, cocoa please*. Blum sits up with a start. She turns left and right, looking for Reza, but Reza isn't there. He didn't want the children to see him lying on the sofa so close to their mother. Only Uma is here, smiling and asking for cocoa.

Breakfast is served in the garden. It is Saturday, and the children have nowhere to be. Blum is sitting at the little table under the cherry tree, reading the newspaper and drinking coffee, watching them play. Everything feels contained. No one suspects her, no one is hunting her down. The only thing weighing on her mind is Massimo. She will phone him, tell him a white lie, and hope he believes her.

The morning sun is dazzling. Blum will sit here for a little while longer and then pack the girls' swimming things. She has promised to take them to the lake and spend the day with them there, in the water, on the meadow beside the banks of the lake, with books. There will be no work and no dead people. It's not a day to spend in front of the computer; that will have to wait until evening. She and Reza will search together for the name that goes with the grinning face. And now a Mercedes turns into the drive.

Schönborn gets out. On this sunny Saturday morning, under the cherry tree, she sees his angry face. He is holding an envelope and sits down with her, just as Blum sat down with him two weeks ago. He lays the envelope in front of her. Then he leans back and raises his face to the sun.

"You're in deep shit."

"No, I'm sitting under a cherry tree. It's perfectly pleasant."

"You have real problems, young lady."

"Do I?"

"Yes. So it would be better if you talked."

"What do you want?"

"I want you to tell me where my son is. Or I'm taking these pictures to the police."

"What pictures?"

"These photographs, here, look."

Blum takes the envelope. It contains photos of a woman with a jack in her hand. They show a car with an open trunk, a casket, and the woman hitting it. There are thirty or forty pictures documenting her fury, every last detail of the murder of Bertl Puch. Blum sits under the cherry tree with the pictures in front of her and Johannes Schönborn opposite. Blum doesn't know what to say. She doesn't know how this man came by them. Did he take the photographs himself, or did he send one of his henchmen, a private detective even? Has someone been watching her, following her every move? Did that person see her leaving Bertl Puch's apartment, luring him into the underground garage, and losing control? Blum has no words to express the turmoil she is in, she can hardly breathe. The children are still playing, running around the yard. Schönborn leans towards her. Blum tries to regain her self-control, react, think of something. She has risen to her feet and she is swaying. She almost falls over but summons all her strength and stands upright.

"You will tell me where my son is."

"Leave me alone."

"No one knows where he is, no one has seen him. It's as if the earth swallowed him up."

"Get lost."

"I've reported him missing, but even the police don't have a clue. There's nothing they can do; his passport has gone, so they say he's probably abroad, but he isn't. I know he isn't."

"I couldn't care less where your son has gone."

"I know you have something to do with it. You'd better pray that he's safe and well."

"You had me watched."

"I did, and it seems that was a very good move. My nose has never yet let me down."

"Get out. Take your damn pictures and fuck off. I don't want you here. Not in my garden and not near my children."

"I'm not going to leave until you tell me where my son is."

"Go away. Now."

"If I go anywhere now it will be straight to the police. Is that what you want?"

"I haven't done anything wrong."

"Not according to these pictures. According to these pictures, you're a murderer."

"All anyone can see in these pictures is a woman with a jack from a tire-changing kit."

"You were hitting out."

"I was furious; I had a flat tire, changing it was tricky."

"You killed him."

"Who?"

"Bertl Puch."

"Nonsense."

"He was in the casket."

"Says who?"

"Says the man who took the photos."

"Well, he's lying."

"He saw Bertl Puch disappear into an underground garage. You had just driven into the garage."

"That's a coincidence. I don't know any Bertl Puch."

"He was a friend of my son. That's no coincidence. Jaunig is dead. Puch is dead. I want to know what you've done to my son."

"Why don't you just go to the police? Let them help you. You're on the wrong track. I have nothing to do with these people."

"You were in Puch's apartment."

"Was I?"

"I have photos showing you entering the building where he lives."

"That must be another coincidence."

"He's dead, isn't he?"

"Who's dead?"

"My son."

"I don't know."

"I'm going to destroy you. I'll take all you have. This house, your children, your life. You will pay."

"I beg to differ. And do you know why? Because you're a greedy, power-hungry old man. You're not going to let a scandal get in the way. I know you want to run this province. You're not about to take risks. And I know what a filthy bastard your son is."

"So he's still alive?"

"I've no idea, but I'd like to show you something. Wait here. I'll be back in a minute."

Blum gets up, goes into the garage, and digs out the photos of the cellar. She has hidden them among the old cross-shaped gravestones, in a crate on the floor. She comes back with the folder and, without another word, hands him the pictures.

"What is this?"

"Art."

"That's my son's watermark."

"Correct. The whole project was thought up by your precious offspring."

"I don't follow."

"Look more closely. Look into the eyes of those women. And the boy. What do you see?"

"What should I see?"

"Horror. Suffering."

"I can't and won't discuss my son's art here. I'm here to talk about my photographs, not his portraits."

"Well, you're wrong. The portraits are precisely the reason why you're here."

"If you don't tell me what you know, I'm going to the police this instant."

"Be my guest. Take these photos of your son's with you, and tell the police that he abducted and imprisoned two women and one man, then took pictures as he raped them. Tell them this went on for five years and your son is a monster."

"What on earth are you talking about?"

"The woman in this photograph told me all about it."

"Nonsense."

"If you feel the need to share those pictures of me, I'll share your son's photos. I'll tell the story told to me by the woman in that picture. Her name was Dunya."

"Where is she?"

"She was abused for five years. She suffered in ways you can't imagine. And then she was killed, just like that, sacrificed so your son could have his fun."

"My son would never do a thing like that. I know my son."

"Not as well as you think. Your fine son has gone off to South America. I imagine that was more appealing than prison."

"That isn't true."

"You know it is."

"Please. Tell me this is all made up."

"I'm afraid I can't."

"It's just not possible."

"That's what I thought too."

"But what do you have to do with it?"

"Your son is also responsible for my husband's murder. So it would be better for you to let sleeping dogs lie. If you don't change your tune, you can say good-bye to your plans for the future."

"I don't know what to say."

"There's also a video."

"A video?"

"A video that shows more than the victims' faces."

"Christ."

"Whoever took those photographs, call them off. If I find that I'm still being photographed, your career is finished. Do you understand?"

He understands. Johannes Schönborn stands up and goes. He leaves the photographs lying there, both his and Blum's. He gets into the car and motions to his chauffeur to drive away. His face is pale. He didn't spend long wondering whether to fight for his son. He has given up. His decision to disown his flesh and blood was made at lightning speed. Johannes Schönborn drives away, out of the garden, away from Blum. The storm has passed, the sea is calm.

Blum sits under the cherry tree, drinking water. She isn't convinced he believes his son has gone to South America without saying good-bye. But never mind, it makes no difference. Johannes Schönborn will keep his mouth shut. He won't do anything that might endanger his career, he won't stick his head above the parapet. He will not let the world know what his son was really like. Johannes Schönborn will go far in politics. Now Blum is going to pack the girls' things: inflatable rafts, towels, swimsuits. Blum is going swimming, and she won't be jumping into an empty pool. She will dive into the water and she will swim.

41

"Hello, I'm at the pool with the children."

"I'm sorry I didn't come round to see you last night. All hell has broken loose."

"It doesn't matter. We'll see each other later."

"Did you miss me?"

"We had a long afternoon's work, Reza and I. Then we drank a glass of wine, and I just passed out on the sofa."

"That's a pity."

"What is?"

"Oh, everything."

"What do you mean?"

"There's so much work, I can't get around to anything else. I'd love to see you. Touch you. But everything's escalating."

"Why, what's going on?"

"I don't want to bother you with this."

"Oh, come on."

"People are disappearing, Blum."

"What do you mean?"

"Well, people are disappearing without a trace. One after another and no one knows why."

"Who's disappeared?"

"Well, we're still looking for Jaunig's body. We've only found his car, it turned up just this side of the Italian border. But there's still no sign of his body. No one knows anything, no one's seen a thing."

"That's strange."

"And then there was that photographer. The son of our parliamentary deputy. He's disappeared into thin air. Now a well-known chef from Kitzbühel has gone missing. Again, he just vanished without a word, no good-byes, nothing."

"So all these people have been reported missing?"

"Yes."

"And you suspect the disappearances are connected?"

"I'm beginning to wonder whether you might have been right all along."

"What do you mean?"

"About that woman you saw in the forensics lab."

"What about her?"

"I promised you I'd look into it again."

"Yes, so you did. And was she murdered?"

"She died of natural causes. But I've dug out the records from back when we interviewed her, and recent events cast a very different light on her story."

"What do you mean?"

"She was talking about a priest, a photographer, and a cook."

"So it's beginning to make sense?"

"I don't know, but I must look into it. It looks as though Mark was right to follow his hunch. Maybe he was right all along, and everything the woman told us was true."

"What did she tell you?"

"You know that already, Blum."

"How would I know?"

"Mark recorded his conversations, and you listened to them."

"Oh—yes."

"I can put two and two together, Blum."

"But perhaps too late in the day."

"I know I should have trusted your gut feeling."

"So Mark was right."

"It would seem so."

"But what happened? Who killed the priest? Where are the missing people?"

"I don't know, Blum, but someone is hell-bent on revenge."

"Revenge?"

"Yes. You know what went on in that cellar. If what the woman said is true, then someone has their reasons."

"But who would do something like that?"

"The woman."

"Her name was Dunya."

"Suppose she killed the three men and then committed suicide?"

"Is that what you think?"

"Can you think of another explanation?"

"No."

"There's something else, Blum."

"What?"

"It's possible that Mark's death wasn't an accident."

"What do you mean? If it wasn't an accident, what was it?"

"Murder. And you could be in danger."

"Me?"

"You'd better be careful, Blum."

"Meaning?"

"Meaning someone may be out to get you."

42

Someone may be out to get you. Blum can still hear Massimo's words ringing in her ears. She is at the lake with the children, who are gurgling with laughter as they splash around in the water surrounded by beach balls and toy ducks. Her phone is wedged between her chin and her collarbone. She was holding Nela above the water while Massimo was on the phone. He sounded genuinely concerned. He really did think that Blum was the next target of the killer who had beheaded Jaunig, who might be responsible for the disappearance of Schönborn and Bertl Puch. But she was safe. Wasn't she?

Nela is making her first attempts at diving. Uma is playing with a green plastic crocodile. Blum has ended the call and is sitting on the side of the children's pool, watching the girls. How carefree they are, what fun they are having in the water. A fat man in red trunks sits down beside her. Suddenly he is there, his skin almost touching hers. His voice is quiet, little more than a whisper. He is Gustav Schrettl, private investigator, he says, and tells her that he saw some interesting things in the course of his last assignment. He tells her what he knows while Nela splashes him with water and giggles. The fat man sitting beside Blum is a greedy fellow; he has dollar signs in his eyes. *You have a lovely villa*, he says. *You have a really nice life. You don't want that nice life to end, do you? No, I'm sure you wouldn't want it to end.* It is such an improbable place for blackmail, this lake. Schrettl is wearing only bathing trunks, no one would think he was threatening Blum, trying to ruin everything. It's absurd. If this were a scene in a film, Blum would have laughed. *What nonsense*, she would have said. But Schrettl is real, and he isn't going away. He says he saw Bertl Puch, Puch briefly tried to sit up before he died. He didn't take a photo of that, but he saw Puch lying in the casket, still moving, before she struck. Schrettl is dangling his feet in the water. He wants her to pay him half a million euros. He is sneering. *You can always sell your nice house. Or your fancy American hearse. Or you can ask your friend the policeman for help. I'm sure he'll understand your situation.* Schrettl grins. A smug little leech in red trunks.

Blum says nothing but lets him talk. Somewhere deep inside her she knew that something like this would happen, that old Schönborn couldn't call off the man who took the photos just like that. Schrettl wants his share, it all makes sense. A bent detective witnesses a crime; instead of clearing the matter up he wants money for his silence. This half-naked joke of a man is demanding half a million euros. *If you want to make a fool of yourself, be my guest, go to the police.* She leans over and looks him in the eye. Her face is close to his, her voice is clear and distinct. *Now leave me alone*, she whispers. He is a leech who has sucked his fill of blood. Now she will take the leech and throw him back into the water.

Blum stands up, gets her children, and leaves. She doesn't want to sit beside him any longer, smelling his breath, hearing his voice. She wants to get away from him; she would like to hold his head underwater and cut off his legs so he couldn't pursue her anymore. What a greedy little bastard. But he doesn't pose a serious problem, she thinks, he only wants a piece of the cake, he wants to peck up a few crumbs she has left on the ground. Blum turns round, walks away, and drives back to the city. She isn't going to feed him. Whatever happens, Schrettl will play no part.

His car is down in the street. For the last two days Blum has been looking out the window, standing behind the curtain, thinking about what will happen next. She doesn't know how she will pull it off. Wherever she goes, he follows. And he too is followed, by the man in the police car who always parks five cars behind. Massimo insisted on police protection for Blum. The men outside the house are preventing her from getting to the man she is after. Benjamin Ludwig.

Reza discovered the actor's identity while Blum was at the lake. He nodded when she got home and led her to the computer. Reza had clicked his way through countless videos on YouTube, excerpts from his films and interviews—the man was certainly in the public eye. Austrian television had done a feature, *At Home with Benjamin Ludwig*. And there was the face of the man who took off his mask just for a moment, that familiar face, that voice. Everyone can see him in his living room, singing "O sole mio." He beams at the camera, his wife and two children beside him. Benjamin Ludwig, the leading television actor, is at home with his family putting on a show for the cameras, a show about his perfect world. How very different it is from the videos recorded in the cellar. But the song is the same, performed with the same ardor. For the past two or three years he has been playing the part of a forester. Every Thursday evening, he walks through the woods with a broad grin on his face, in a tale of love and pain that attracts millions of viewers. His star is in the ascendancy and his ratings are high. This is the huntsman who aimed his gun at Youn. Who embraces and kisses his wife for the camera. Soon they will go and get Benjamin Ludwig, they will find a way.

But Blum is stuck. There's Schrettl in his car, and there's the policeman in his car. Massimo is penning her in because he wants to protect her. Dear Massimo. Even if their relationship has cooled off now, he is still there for her, having her guarded round the clock. Until he discovers the truth, the police officer will watch over her. She takes him coffee. The police officer unwittingly prevents Schrettl from harassing her anymore. Everything is at a standstill. For the last two days she hasn't left the house. But at least Blum has had time to think. She and Reza spend two days planning their next step. They have found out where Benjamin Ludwig lives, the location of the villa from the TV show. It is an idyllic spot on a slope, apart from the other houses; they have seen it on Google Earth. And they have found out that he is not filming at the moment, he is at home with his family, the media reports. Reza and Blum have made calls, telling lies, they have spent two evenings on the sofa planning their next move, their trip to Munich, down to the last detail. What to do about Schrettl and the policeman. What to do with Benjamin Ludwig. It's a crazy adventure, but that's how Blum likes it. Reza is standing beside her. She looks down at the street and says *Let's go*.

43

Before Schrettl and the police officer can start their engines, they have got away. Down the street with the motorcycle engine roaring. Blum is riding the bike and Reza sits behind her, his arms round her waist, clinging on. This absolutely wouldn't do, he said at first, but then he let her talk him round. The Ducati flies out of the drive, past Schrettl and the police car. They are too fast to be stopped. The motorcycle comes out of nowhere and simply disappears. Their destination remains a mystery. Schrettl will probably be cursing, the police officer will be phoning Massimo to say he has let her out of his sight, going he doesn't know where, with a man riding shotgun. Blum is in high spirits as she accelerates and overtakes, but she knows where the speed cameras are, she knows where to be careful. There's only Blum and the highway and the hands on her waist. In an hour and twenty minutes they reach Munich.

No one has stopped them. They ride to the airport and leave the bike in the parking lot. It is ten in the morning and they take the S-Bahn into the city and then the bus to Bogenhausen. This is where the rich people live, Benjamin Ludwig among them. They have little to carry, only a rucksack with the bare essentials; they hope to be back in Innsbruck by evening. In twelve hours' time it should all be over. All they have planned, sitting in the S-Bahn like two children on a day out. But Blum is no longer alone in the adventure. And it feels good, right, to be conspiring with this quiet man she has known for years. But he has never been as close to her as he is now. Blum knows that he wouldn't hesitate for a moment if they got into trouble. *Ludwig will talk,* Reza has assured her. He has promised to make sure that she gets the rest of the story. She will find out who was at the wheel of the car that killed Mark. She will know everything there is to know about the five men. Only then will her mind be at rest.

They make their way through Munich like tourists, without exchanging a word. Reza and Blum have made it to the slope; Ludwig's garden is in their sights. Like thieves, they hide behind trees for hours on end, because Ludwig isn't home. No children, no wife, just an empty house in Bogenhausen. The information that Ludwig's production company gave them is incorrect. With every hour that passes, they doubt themselves more. All they can do is wait. Massimo keeps phoning, and Blum gives evasive answers. He is worried about her. Afternoon comes, then evening, and they hold out hope that the family has just gone shopping, that they will come round the corner and they can put their plan into action at last. But that doesn't happen. When darkness falls, the house is still empty. And Blum is hungry. She worries about the children, she is tired and impatient, she wants to get this over and done with. She begins to resent Reza's silence. He has hardly said a word all day. He just sits beside her, staring at the house. Blum has no idea what is going through his head, but he doesn't share her annoyance at the wasted day. His face is calm, devoid of stormy weather. Reza has a task, to wait for Benjamin Ludwig, and he will not move from his post an inch until the task is complete. Blum knows that he would sit there all night, so she persuades him to come with her down the hill, to find a hotel with a restaurant. Blum wants to rest, to take her mind off Ludwig, Dunya, and Mark just for a while. She wants to draw breath, make a short phone call to Karl, and have a drink. *Tomorrow is another day,* she says.

Reza and Blum are at the reception desk of a small hotel. Blum doesn't stop to think, *A double room for one night, please* comes out quite naturally. Instinct tells her that it is the right thing to do. She doesn't want to be alone and he says nothing; there is a quiet under-standing between them. Reza will stay with her. Here he is at the bar beside her, because Blum doesn't feel like sleeping yet, and she is worried about the children. She has phoned Karl and told him she will be back later than expected, has asked him to look after the children overnight and for the day tomorrow. Karl doesn't say yes immediately, as he usually would. He hesitates. Something is wrong; she senses that he had other plans. But Karl doesn't want to upset Blum by refusing. *We'll manage all right,* he says. *Don't worry, Blum. You do whatever it is you have to do and then come home.* Then he ends the call, leaving her with Reza.

They are together at the bar, because she still doesn't feel like sleep-ing. She isn't ready to go to their room and lie down beside him. They don't talk about the room or her need not to be alone. Reza makes it easy for her, acting as if it were the most normal thing in the world, as if they were friends who just happen to be sharing a room. He orders wine for Blum and beer for himself. With every sip he becomes more talkative. Reza respects her request not to mention Ludwig, so he talks about the children, new models of casket, their plans to renovate the preparation room. It feels good to be talking and drinking in a hotel somewhere in Bogenhausen. Benjamin Ludwig isn't important. Nothing is important, noth-ing hurts them, nothing threatens them. They drink glass after glass, and everything is simple and easy. Reza makes Blum laugh. They remember the lighter moments of their profession, eccentric wishes, difficult family members. They remember all that they have shared in the last seven years, their time in the preparation room, the countless dead bodies they have collected, the funerals they have attended. Reza was always by her side. Reza orders more wine, more beer, and he smiles, and the smile does her good. There is more between them than work. Blum puts her arms round him. *Come on, come and dance with me.*

They dance in the little hotel bar, skirting the tables and chairs. Although Reza can't dance, he lets her win him over. Briefly, he protests, but then he goes along with her. Blum beams at him. She just wants to dance, close her eyes, let him lead her, listen to the music in his arms, sense whether he can hold her properly. It would never have entered Blum's head to think of Reza as more than a colleague, a friend, her husband's protégé. It never occurred to her that he might touch her, that their breath might mingle. They turn on the dance floor, slowly. Reza moves carefully past the bar furniture, holding Blum in his arms, her head on his shoulder.

Upstairs they glide, with another bottle of wine—just in case— through the door and into the little bedroom. Blum disappears into the bathroom for a moment, and he sits on the bed. Night has fallen in Bogenhausen. Blum comes out of the bathroom and stands in front of him. Reza doesn't move. He holds the bottle silently, staring up at her. Blum stands there, naked.

44

Blum does all the talking. If Benjamin Ludwig says one word, one of his children will die. He knows Blum is serious. Reza shot at the tree which Ludwig was standing next to, a bullet is lodged in the trunk. The impact was brief and barely audible, but it was quite enough to show Benjamin Ludwig that the people on the hill mean business. They are going to shoot one of his children—then both of them, if he doesn't keep his mouth shut. Blum tells him what he is to do. He is to listen. She tells him what she knows and then she threatens him. *First I will kill the boy. Then the girl. Then your wife, then you.*

How happy the family looked in the garden. Reza and Blum didn't have long to wait. Ludwig turned up ten minutes ago, soon after they arrived back behind their tree. The children ran to their swing, his wife went into the house.

Ludwig stands there, as if rooted to the spot. The children are calling to him, wanting him to join them, to push them high in the air on the swing. The good father who takes care of his children, the good father who raped a child. Youn was seventeen when they put him in the cellar. Blum has listened again to everything Dunya had to say about the huntsman. What he, Benja-

239

min Ludwig, did to them. Now Benjamin Ludwig listens to what Blum has to say, with his phone to his ear and his eyes searching the slope. But he doesn't say another word; he is afraid of hearing another shot. The gun has a silencer, no one heard the first shot, no one can help him. There is only Blum's voice telling him to pack a bag and take his passport with him, to say good-bye to his wife and children. He must think up some pretext, she tells him, invent a reason for his sudden departure. *Lie to them. Now, go into the house, pack your things, say good-bye, and come back out. Then get into your fucking car.*

When she saw it, Blum struggled to breathe. The Rover, here. She hadn't expected to see that car ever again. But there it was, outside the house, with children clambering out of the backseat. Blum ends the call and Ludwig disappears into the house. For a few minutes she and Reza are alone. Together with her fury and hatred, she has the sudden answer to her question. Who was driving the car? Who killed Mark? The car really exists, it was in Bavaria all along. It belongs to a world that was still intact. There it is, in front of her, coming down the road.

Her husband's murderer is sitting in front of her, his overnight bag is on the backseat. Ludwig has done as she told him. He emerged from the house after four minutes, his wife was standing in the doorway waving good-bye. Benjamin Ludwig was in a hurry; he had to make sure the children were out of firing range, he had to protect them and his wife. He had to do as Blum said. He stopped, and they got in. The pistol is in Reza's hand. Blum has no idea where it came from. They discussed their need for a gun and the gun materialized. *I'll see to that,* Reza had said. Now the gun is in his hand, forcing Benjamin Ludwig to drive towards Starnberg. He is silent, still: Blum doesn't want to hear his lies and excuses, she doesn't want to hear him beg, whimper, or wail. There's only the gun in his back, the past, and Reza by her side.

All night, her naked body lay against his. She just wanted to feel his skin, to undress him, disappear in him, plunge into him, and let herself fall. She would have let it happen with a clear conscience, she would have taken and given everything, because she thought it was time to give him something in return. Something like love, a sense of gratitude. She was curious too. Blum wanted to know what he would smell like, what his tongue would taste like moving in her mouth. What his hands would do as he thrust into her. She wanted to feel him, all of him, continue dancing with their eyes closed. But ten hours ago, his eyes said *no*.

Benjamin Ludwig drives through the city. Reza gives him directions; they have to make a stop before they reach the lake. They need cartons, plastic wrap, and sticky tape. They stop in the parking lot of a DIY store, one car in a sea of cars. Reza hands Blum the gun and goes into the store, leaving Blum alone with Ludwig. The actor and the undertaker sit in silence for ten long minutes. He is too afraid to turn around, he feels the barrel of the gun in his back. Blum is pressing it firmly against him. She would like to pull the trigger, eliminate him just like that, send this man who looks squeaky clean to hell, tell the world what he is really like, what he's done. She wants to kill him here and now, in the parking lot of some shopping mall in Munich. She would like to hurt him, tell him she loved the man he ran over and killed, that he meant everything to her: Mark, the father of her children. She thinks of him playing with Uma and Nela in the yard. A family that isn't a family anymore. It would take only a second to kill him. A single shot and it would be over. Now, before Reza comes back to stow his purchases in the trunk. Before he gets back into the car and tells Ludwig to drive on.

But they get the TV star to chauffeur them to Starnberg as though it is the most normal thing in the world. Slowly, they skirt the lake. Summer is over, many of the houses stand empty. Rich people's villas, boathouses, holiday homes. Reza directs him; they are looking for the perfect house, a house with a driveway they can disappear down in broad daylight. No one will notice. It will just be an expensive car parked outside an expensive house, three people getting out of the car and going down to the water through a large backyard. There's only a fence to be climbed; they carry their rucksack, bags, and cartons with them. Reza, Blum, and Ludwig are quite the trio. He walks ahead of them and keeps turning round, looking for a way of escape. Because he knows that this is the end, the end of everything.

When Reza fell asleep, his fingers stayed on Blum's skin. He was tipsy and tired. She didn't move, she wanted to stay close to him and not move an inch. It was for the best that he turned her down, that he didn't just accept her body, her mouth, her breasts. She would have followed through, she wanted to. But Reza just took her hand and looked at her. Blum could see how much he liked her. He wanted her, but he restrained himself.

But now there is no restraint or embarrassment, now he is Blum's faithful little soldier, functioning like a machine. He forces the lock and opens the door. There's no alarm, only a beautiful old boathouse that has lain untouched for weeks. It is the perfect place to talk to Ludwig. No one will hear him; the house next door stands empty too, and on the other side of the boathouse there is only woodland. It won't matter how long and loud he screams. Reza spreads a tarpaulin on the floor as if he were about to lay the table. He takes tools out of his rucksack, places the sticky tape and plastic wrap within reach. The preparations are over quickly, giving Ludwig no time to work out what is going to happen next. He hops from one foot to the other, wanting to run far and fast, but the gun in Blum's hand prevents this.

She didn't sleep all night. She didn't want the feeling to stop, didn't want Reza to get up and leave her. She wanted to go on feeling it as long as possible, until morning when he opened his eyes and began caressing her back again. Reza carried on where he had left off. But then she said it was time to go back to the house and to the nightmare. Now Reza is hitting him with an oar and tying him up with sticky tape, binding his hands and feet. Night is mingling with day, life with Mark is mingling with her life now. A life in which people die, and die when she wants them to.

Blum stands there watching as if she had nothing to do with it, as if she were a rubbernecker at an accident, eager to satisfy her curiosity. The boathouse contains a row boat, a small launch with an electric motor, and Benjamin Ludwig, who is screaming. He has come round and can feel the sticky tape, realizes how hopeless his situation is. He can't control himself any longer, he has to act. First he curses, insulting them. Then he calms down, breathes deeply in and out, and pulls himself together. The actor is rehearsing before he comes onstage to play his part and tell the truth. He will try to save his life by talking, because he guesses what is coming, because he knows the others are dead or have disappeared. Because he knows that these two mean business. He can read that in Blum's face, nothing in her features gives him reason to hope. All he can do is talk and speak nothing but the truth. *If you lie to me you're dead.* She is sitting on the floor beside him, the gun in her hand. She is very close now. She presses the barrel to Ludwig's forehead.

While Blum talks to him, Reza moves away. *You will answer my questions. Keep your answers short and to the point. I won't ask twice.* His questions remain unanswered. *What are you going to do to me? What do you want from me? Why are you doing this? Where are Schönborn and Puch? You abducted them. Are they still alive? Are they dead?* But Blum's gun is against his forehead and she wants the truth about the cellar: where it is, how it came to be, why five men decided to throw off their inhibitions and act like animals, brutes who observed no rules. Blum wants to know, something in her wants to comprehend the incomprehensible, understand how such a thing can come to pass, a place where anything went, a place which traded on violence and humiliation, punishment and penance. How it lasted five long years. *The cellar is in Kitzbühel. It is underneath the restaurant. I own the house, it was our holiday home. We converted it. It was Puch's idea. We were drunk at the time. He thought it all up. We would eat well then play games in the cellar. Five men realizing a dream. Five lucky men.*

Blum's desire to pull the trigger grows with every word he speaks. Click. A gunshot, then nothing. But Blum wants more. She wants to know where the boy is and whether he is still alive. What they have done with him. *I don't know. I really don't know. The cellar has been cleared, the furniture and cages have been thrown away. It's all gone, the place is empty. There's nothing left. I don't know where the boy is. I don't know. You must believe me. He disappeared into thin air.* So nothing remains in Kitzbühel, nothing to prove the nightmare was real apart from photographs and videos. And the words of Benjamin Ludwig. It is a sad truth, and it confirms what she already knows. That he hunted them, shot darts at them, always singing that song. Because those men crossed a line and couldn't go back, so they carried on. They made the madness part of their lives and justified it to themselves. *We always fed them well. It was good for them to be anesthetized. That way it didn't hurt. They were no better off where they*

came from. We looked after them well. They had everything they needed.
They were well off with us.

Blum wants to kick him as hard as she can, until he shuts up. She
wants to make him feel the horror, the unimaginable cruelty of
every encounter. Blum wants him to say that he is sorry, that he
knows he is a monster. She wants to punish him and eliminate
him, and then she wants more. She wants the answer to her final
question, the conclusion of the confession, though there is no forgiveness to be had. Who did it? Was it him? Did he drive the car?
Was he at the wheel of the Rover? Or was it one of the others?

"You killed my husband."
"I did what?"
"You know exactly who I am. Admit it or you're dead."
"Yes. I know who you are."
"It was your car."
"But I didn't kill your husband."
"Don't lie to me."
"I'm not."
"It was your car."
"But I wasn't driving."
"Then who was?"
"Not me."
"Then who?"
"You're not going to like this."
"Either you tell me or you die."
"He was driving."
"The clown?"
"Yes, the clown."
"Who is he and where can I find him? Open your fucking mouth
and tell me the truth."

"He's to blame, not me. For the whole thing. He killed the girl. And your husband too. He said it had to be done. We tried to talk him out of it, believe me."

"His name. I want his name."

"He wanted me to do it, but I said I couldn't kill your husband. He tried to insist. He said we'd all go to prison if he didn't die."

"Ten . . . nine . . ."

"It's his fault, not mine."

"His name."

"I didn't want anyone to die! I only let him use my car. I'm not responsible, I could never kill anyone."

"Five . . . four . . ."

"You have no idea who you're dealing with."

"Three."

"He'll kill you too."

"Two."

"He won't hesitate for a moment."

"One."

"His name is Massimo. And he's a police—"

Blum fires the gun. Her finger pulls the trigger and now his head is lolling to the side. *His name is Massimo.* A few seconds ago, he was breathing, and now he is dead. But Blum can still hear him. *His name is Massimo.* The name eats a hole in her, fast and deep, it hollows her out, takes away all she still has. *His name is Massimo.* Blum sits down. She can't think; she feels sick. To think he said that name, Massimo, the last name she was expecting. Sitting on the floor, leaning back against the wooden wall, she hears it again. It echoes around her head, even though she has pressed Stop. *His name is Massimo.* Blum doesn't move. She can't do anything but sit there, looking at Ludwig's corpse. She cannot grasp what he said. Reza is slowly kneeling down in front of her. He carefully takes her face in his hands. *We can get through this*, he says, his fingers on her cheeks. They keep her from falling.

Ludwig said *He'll kill you too*. Reza kisses her on the forehead and stands up. *Stay where you are*. Then he sets to work on Ludwig the way they have planned it. Calmly, Reza dissects him and packages him up. All is quiet in the boathouse as the blood runs into the lake. Blum is lost for words, she can't help Reza, she can't move, because she can feel Massimo, deep inside her, his hands on her body, his tongue. Massimo who rooted around inside her, lied to her, stole into her. *His name is Massimo*. Her husband's best friend was one of those five men. *The clown was the worst of them all*, Dunya had said. Blum had slept with him. Blum can't move.

Reza saws off Ludwig's leg. He is using a handsaw and an ax. It is heavy work; there is no current here, so he cannot use power tools. Reza is sweating. But he doesn't mind that Blum can't help him. *I can manage*, he says. The leg is wrapped tight with plastic wrap, then sticky tape, then it goes into a carton, then more tape. Arms, torso, head, Reza packages them all up. Then he will clean up and carry Ludwig to the car; they will leave the boathouse exactly as they found it. There will be nothing to show that a man died here. The blood is in the lake, there's only a broken padlock that will be blamed on local youths. No one will suspect a thing. Ludwig is ready to be dispatched. The packages are addressed to the Funerary Institute; Reza has chosen a haulage firm close to the airport. They will pass it before leaving Ludwig's car in the underground garage at the airport; they will wear gloves and leave no prints. Then they will get straight back on the motorcycle and return to Innsbruck. Tomorrow, Ludwig will arrive in the post. They will store him in the cool room, divide him between caskets, and before Massimo's eyes, Ludwig will disappear without a trace.

247

Does he know it's Blum? He must have seen Dunya in her house, he knows that she hasn't let up in her investigations. Does he think she's capable of it? She can't say. Was the plainclothes officer in the car outside her house there to follow her, not protect her? Massimo has been checking up on her, for the last few hours her phone hasn't stopped ringing. He spoke into her voice mail in tones of concern. Mark's murderer sounded so friendly. But he has her in his sights.

Back on the highway, Reza rides the bike and Blum sits behind him. She puts her arms around his waist, her head rests on his back, under her helmet tears fall. She feels empty, she wants to get home and wash away the thought of Massimo. She can't believe how simple it was, how stupid, how blind she had been. Everything is falling into place. Dunya disappeared after Blum slept with him. He must have taken another look in the children's room; he must have seen her in Nela's bed, the woman he had defiled for years. Dunya could have brought the whole house of cards toppling down, just like Mark could. So Massimo executed her too. He held her head underwater, and then he kissed Blum.

45

Uma is on his lap. Nela holds him from behind. At first Blum thinks it's Karl. She is surprised that they're not upstairs with him, that he is in their room instead. She stole quietly along the corridor to surprise them, craving a brief moment of family life after all that has happened. She wanted to hear her children's laughter, see their pink cuddly toys, feel their innocence wash over her. She wanted to be a mother, not a murderer.

Blum stands in the doorway. *Mama is back*, she cries. And then her voice dies away. She is rooted to the spot, staring at Massimo. He smiles at her and puts Uma down on the floor. Blum tries to smile back but panic has seized her. All the same, she reacts fast. *What a surprise!* She doesn't move but opens her arms wide and gathers her children into them. *Mama, Mama, Mama.* Kneeling down, she hugs them, avoiding his eyes. She doesn't know what to do, she thinks hard, she wants to get them to safety, away from this man. Out of the room, out of the house, far away. She sees his hands on her children but she knows he mustn't suspect that anything is amiss, that she knows the truth. She must act as though nothing has changed. There must be no fear, no trembling until he has left the house. *How nice to see you*, then she stands up and gives him a hug. Her whole body shrinks from it, but she puts her arms around the man who killed her husband. She does it for the children. She'd have given anything for him to go away before showing his true colors, before turning into a beast. So she smiles and she pretends. She sits the children down in front of the television and leads him into the living room.

"What are you doing here, Massimo?"

"Karl phoned. He had to go to the dentist."

"He didn't mention it."

"You know that I'm happy to look after the girls. I enjoy their company."

"Karl was supposed to be looking after them."

"Like I said, I was happy to take the reins. But tell me, where have you been? I was worried sick."

"I had to get out of here. I just rode around on the bike—I had cabin fever."

"So you were away overnight?"

"Yes."

"On your own?"

"Yes."

"My colleague told me Reza was with you."

"I gave him a lift into the city. Then I went my own way."

"Where is he?"

"Who?"

"Reza."

"Why would I know?"

"There's something the matter with him. Where did you take him?"

"Are you interrogating me?"

"No."

"Then stop asking me so many questions. I only wanted a few hours on my own. Reza is fine."

"And I only want you to be safe, Blum. I told you, you're probably in danger. How am I going to keep an eye on you if you run off like that?"

"Nothing's going to happen to me."

"Your children need you."

"I'm quite aware of that."

"Did you understand me, Blum?"

"Yes."

"I don't know how many times I called you."

"Sorry."

"I don't want anything to happen to you."

"I have no intention of letting anything happen to me."

"I'll look after you, Blum."

"I know you will. But now I must see to the girls. I'll call you, I promise."

"When?"

"Tomorrow."

"I'd like to spend some time with you, Blum."

"And I'd like to see you too."

"You would?"

"Yes."

"What shall we do?"

"Anything you like."

"Anything?"

"Yes, but I wish you'd send your man home. You being here for me is quite enough."

"When tomorrow?"

"Once the girls are asleep."

"Where?"

"I'll call you. And—thanks for looking after them."

"Please don't go running off again."

"No, I won't go running off. I'll stay at home like a good girl until you catch the villains."

"Blum?"

"Yes?"

"You know I'd leave Ute like a shot, don't you?"

"Yes, I know."

"Your children need a father."

"Let me mull this over."

"You're so beautiful, Blum."

"But it's time for you to go. Please."

"See you tomorrow?"

"Yes, tomorrow."

What a bastard. The way he grins, trying to crawl into her favor. The way he threatens her implicitly, letting her know he won't let her out of his sight. Blum can hardly stay on her feet, she's exhausted herself, suppressing her fury, dissimulating, saying things she hates herself for. The lying bastard. She pictures him going downstairs, the front door opening and closing. Blum runs to her children. He's never going to lay a finger on Uma or Nela again. Blum is determined never again to fear for her children's safety; Massimo will never set eyes on them again. Uma and Nela are absorbed in the screen; they want to stay in its colorful world, they barely notice Blum's kisses. They have no time for anxiety, tears, or fear. *Can we watch a little more, Mama? A little more, please.* They are only children watching television, children untouched by the world, who think they have nothing to fear. This is a day like any other because Massimo is part of their lives, a family friend, a man whose lap they have sat on countless times. They kissed him good-bye on the cheek, then went back to the little penguins on the screen. Massimo has gone, he has left the house, and he's never going to set foot in it again.

Blum is breathing steadily in and out. For a moment she just stands there, wondering how she will do it and where, and what must happen first. She wonders what she is going to say to the fat little man in the red trunks, because he's still there, parked outside her house, and he is still demanding money. As she goes downstairs she searches for the words that will make him go away. While the girls watch TV, spellbound, she will take care of that little problem. Blum goes through the front garden, down the drive, and into the road where Mark died. Schrettl is in his car: she will tap on the window and tell him that she will kill him if he stays where he is.

Just one sentence will do because she is furious enough to leave havoc in her wake, because Massimo touched the children, because she slept with him, because Mark is dead, because nothing is as it was. She was happy before that car came along. She doesn't wait for a cue, she simply leans in and tells him she will kill him. *If you don't clear out I'll kill you*, in a voice as cold as ice. He knows that she means it, it is written in her eyes, in her mouth. She isn't joking, she will carry out her threats. She sees his confusion, his uncertainty. Schrettl and Blum look at each other for ten seconds, then Blum removes her head from the car window and leaves without a backward glance. Behind her an engine starts. Schrettl's car glides down the street.

Blum goes upstairs and sits down with the children. Her head is almost bursting with noise. She must act fast. She sits on the sofa with the girls and stares ahead. Maya the Bee is flying across the screen and Massimo is a murderer. Blum must talk to Reza and they must get rid of Massimo. Because he suspects Reza and because she saw doubt in his eyes. He may know more than he admits and she cannot bear for him to live a day longer. His presence is like poison. He took Mark away from her, he tore out her heart with his bare hands.

Blum remembers everything she knows about the clown. Dunya told her he was the worst, the most sadistic, the most violent. He had joined about a year after it started, and his arrival made the cellar an even more brutal place. Four tormentors became five. And Dunya was more afraid of him than of the others. Massimo, the kindly police officer, the helpful family friend, Blum's admirer, the unhappy husband—no one would ever have thought that he could beat and rape a pregnant woman until she was about to lose her baby and die of pain. Dunya had told them, first Mark and then Blum, how he punched Ilena in the stomach with his fist again and again, punching the child, perhaps even his own. Every last detail had been recorded on Mark's phone. The clown humiliated and beat them. Sometimes he didn't rape them, he just beat them, laughing crazily, a man out of control. He would take Dunya's head and slam it on the floor when she didn't go along with what he wanted or give him a smile. *Give me a smile, slut. I said you have to give me a smile. Do you think you're too good for me?* He would take her by the hair and smash her head on the plush red carpet until Dunya would lose consciousness and he would walk away.

Massimo, the kindly soul, the man who upheld the law. He spent nights on end in the garage with Mark, drinking beer, slapping him on the back, relaxing after work. Blum still couldn't comprehend why Massimo had sought the company of Jaunig, Schönborn, and Puch. And Ludwig. Why he had gone off to a cellar with those men, how he could have been capable of those things.

The filthy bastard. Blum couldn't call him anything else. The epithet kept rising to her lips while Maya's friend the lazy bee Willy was sucking up honey on the screen. While Uma and Nela giggled and nestled close to her. *Filthy bastard. Massimo. I'll see you dead if it's the last thing I do.*

46

Slowly she opens her eyes. Very slowly, because she knows what is coming. She doesn't want to see what's there but she can smell it and hear it. The disinfectant, the sound of the cooling unit, the buzzing of the old neon tube above her head to the left, the crane they use to lift corpses into caskets. Blum knows exactly where she is. She doesn't know how she got there, but she knows she is in the preparation room. She knows that someone has knocked her out, undressed her, and tied her to the table. The aluminum is cold against her skin. She tries to reconstruct what has happened and work out what is going to happen next. She can move only her head. She turns it one way then the other, looking around for help. She tries to scream, but all she hears is groaning; her lips are covered in tape. She doesn't want to take it in; doesn't want to see him there beside her.

It is Reza's blood on the table, pooling around his headless torso. Reza is dead, Reza can no longer help her. Only flesh remains. She thinks of the last thing he said. He was still embracing her, their hands had touched. Now Reza's limbs are strewn on the floor. He has done to Reza what she did to others, he has mimicked her. Blum screams but no one can hear her from under the sticky tape. She tosses her head back and forth, trying to catch a glimpse of him, but she can't. If he's in the room she should be able to hear him, but silence reigns. He's in the house, she knows it, he's waiting for her to wake. He's with the children, with Karl. Blum pictures what he is doing to them. She tries to break free, she can't bear the thought, she must protect her little angels. This can't be happening—she hears him. He is in the room. He is getting up from his chair and coming towards her.

His footsteps approach; the sound of his breathing comes closer. He is taking his time; he wants to torment her, wants to make her suffer. He stops, pausing to watch her rib cage rise and fall. He is toying with her, listening to her heart beat faster and faster, seeing her wrists twitch as her fingers try to find an escape. Blum is naked on the table, her skin and breasts exposed. How long has she been lying here, Blum wonders, how long has he been staring at her? What has he done to her while she's been asleep? He has taken off her clothes, cut them from her body. Perhaps he has packed them up like a present. Every thought hurts now she is at his mercy, now she is no longer at the helm. The boat is drifting on a shark-infested sea.

Blum knows she is going to die. Her mind has reached a still point, she is submitting to what will happen next. She no longer tries to escape, she just lies there, staring at the ceiling, trying not to think of the children. She won't, she can't. The children are okay, he won't hurt the children. There's only the buzz of the cooling unit, the hum of the neon tubes, the white of the ceiling, and her memories. Never mind what's coming, never mind what happens to her, she will think of the good times. She will think of Mark, his hands on her belly just before Uma was born.

"I'm afraid, Mark."
"What of?"

"Of what's inside me."

"There's nothing to fear. We're in this together, Blum. Nothing bad will happen."

"But everything's about to change."

"Change is good."

"Why?"

"When winter is over the trees turn green."

It does her good to think of Mark, of what he said and how he looked at her three years ago. *The trees turn green.* And how he kissed her. Never mind what happens next. Mark is beside her, very close. Never mind what happens, he holds her in his arms.

She looks away, to the ceiling, because he is coming closer now. The broad grin looms over her, the brightly colored plastic mouth. Only his eyes say she reacted too slowly, that the tables have been turned. Massimo is two eyes and a mask. He has won. She sees him approach, whispering softly, just loud enough for her to hear. *None of this had to happen, Blum. None of it, do you understand? Everything would have been all right. We could have been together.* There's just her fear and his familiar voice as he bids her farewell, almost lovingly, as he tells her it is over. He loved her, he says, he would have done anything for her. She watches as he removes the mask and takes her face firmly in his hands. For twenty long seconds, he presses his lips onto the tape which covers her lips. Then he stabs her. Blum does not move.

47

Blum has spent all night here on the preparation table, not moving but breathing. Her rib cage rises and falls and her eyes are open wide. She has spent a night imagining what he might do to her, tormenting herself. She spent the afternoon with the children, ate supper with them and Reza, then she came down here, locked the door, and lay down with her thoughts. She imagined the worst: Massimo twisting the knife into her, dissecting Reza. What it would be like, what he would do to her: a nightmare that will come true if she doesn't act at once. She can't wait any longer, she can't risk it. She doesn't want to find out what he knows and what he doesn't know. She can't give him the chance to investigate, to become suspicious of Reza. She must end it all before his lips come down on hers. Blum will have to call him and arrange a meeting. She will speak to him as soon as it is light in two hours' time. She must keep the upper hand, strike before he can. She and Reza will move faster or else they will both die.

For hours she has been lying there with the naked body of an old woman on the preparation table beside her. She must see to the old woman first. As she pushes cotton wool into the woman's nostrils, as she washes and blow-dries her hair, as she cleans the dirt from under her fingernails, Blum considers how she will dispatch

Massimo. She doesn't want him to die painlessly; she wants to punish and execute him. In her mind she searches for a place where she can dispose of him, because she doesn't want him to set foot in her house again. There must be an alternative. As she stitches up the old woman's mouth she plans Massimo's death. She will discuss it with Reza over breakfast; together they will find a way. They will put the old woman in her casket and wait for her family, and then they will wait for evening. Blum will read the girls a bedtime story and kiss them good night. She will make sure that they are safe. She'll do anything for that. And that is why she calls Massimo's number once it is morning. She breathes deeply in and out three times. Then she hears his voice. Friendly, eager.

"Blum, how good to hear from you."

"And you."

"I didn't expect you to call so soon."

"I said I'd like to see you."

"When?"

"Well, I'd like to see you straightaway, but I have work to do. And then there are the children. Shall we meet this evening? Are you free?"

"For you, always."

"I'd like to be alone with you."

"I'm glad to hear that, Blum."

"But where? I wouldn't want the children to find you in my bed."

"Come round to mine."

"But what about Ute?"

"She's not here."

"Where is she?"

"Away."

"What do you mean? Away where?"

"My wife drank two bottles of schnapps, then tried to kill herself."

"Oh! When?"

"A week ago."

"Why didn't you say?"

"It wouldn't have changed anything."

"What happened?"

"She cut her wrists in the bath."

"Where is she now?"

"In a psychiatric hospital."

"I'm so sorry."

"There's no need."

"And when is she coming home?"

"No one knows."

"We can put it off, Massimo. I understand if you'd rather be alone now."

"No, come and see me this evening."

"About nine?"

"You're making me very happy, Blum."

"Kisses to you, and see you later."

She had to grit her teeth to say those things; she hates herself for every word she said to lead him on. She throws her phone at the wall with all her might and it crashes to the floor. Then she suppresses a scream. She doesn't want anyone to hear her; she just wants this to stop, for Massimo's heart to stop. Good old Massimo.

She wants him to be as lively as the woman on the table in front of her. Blum has dressed her brightly, in the traditional Austrian way: a white blouse, an apron, a pearl necklace, her hair braided into a wreath. Blum has manipulated her lips into a smile. She remembers how close Mark and Massimo were. She doesn't want him suspecting, not for a moment, that anything is wrong, that nothing more is on the agenda than a little bit of fucking in the marital bed. On the dining table, in the bathtub where Ute almost bled to death, never mind where. All he wants is to get his prick into silly little Blum. She is the ultimate conquest, his best friend's wife. She senses how much he wants her. *You're making me very happy.* The bastard.

48

There is no going back. She considers the chances of being seen, of dying, of spending the rest of her life behind bars. She can't rule out any of those possibilities, but still, they won't deter her. They are doing the right thing; Blum is convinced, and so is Reza. He will do whatever it takes, for Mark and for Blum. He is lying under a rug in the back, waiting for the vehicle to stop. Blum is driving straight to Massimo's house in the hearse. Not the Cadillac, the minibus. They don't want to attract attention. There is a casket in the back, the cheapest they have.

She drives slowly to the quiet, upscale suburb on the outskirts of the city. Ute and Massimo had a new house built in this residential community just a little less than seven years ago, back when everything seemed all right. Ute hadn't taken to the bottle, they believed the trampoline in their backyard would be used, that they had a future together. Mark and Blum had been here so often for barbecues, she remembers the cheerful summer evenings they spent at their friends' home. Ute had insisted on green paint, so it stands out from the others. The garage is open. Blum has called him again and asked him to leave the gate unlocked. She said she didn't want to be seen visiting, not after what happened to Ute. She doesn't want people to talk.

She turns off the engine and closes the gate from inside. Reza will stay in the vehicle until Blum is in the house and Massimo is in her arms. Then he will get out, go quietly up to the house, and hit him over the head with an iron bar. Once he is unconscious on the floor, they will tie him up with sticky tape, gag him, and put him in the casket. Then they will wind blankets around him, and more tape around the casket, to make sure there is no chance of escape.

Her doubts and fears surge back. Massimo is a police officer, it is his job to be suspicious. Perhaps he has suspected that she won't come alone, that Reza might be with her. What if he meets her with a gun in his hand? What if he hears Reza approach? What if he pulls away from Blum and avoids Reza's blow? Blum pictures it all: the iron bar flying through the air, Massimo fighting back, overpowering Reza.

Blum opens the door. She mustn't think like this. Down a small corridor she goes, and straight into the house. She calls his name; she is afraid, she can hear her heart thudding. She hears her heart and then his voice, coming from the kitchen. *Come on in. I've got us a nice bottle of red.* He stands in front of her, looking innocent, just a man with a bottle in his hand and the corkscrew he has used to open it. He fills two glasses while Blum stands in the doorway, smiling. She forces herself to walk over and embrace him, to kiss him on the neck. She is giving herself time; he mustn't suspect a thing. Tenderly, she puts her lips to his filthy skin. *It's lovely to be alone, just the two of us*, she whispers, turning her head. She doesn't want this intimacy to last a second longer, but she must run no risks. She scans the room for any sign of danger, anything that looks out of place. She examines his face too, looks into his eyes and does not turn her own away. There is still time for her to run. But the face that looks back at her is the face of Mark's best friend, not that of a crazed man in a mask. Everything is all right for now.

Massimo goes ahead into the living room and Blum follows. She must get him to put some music on, otherwise he'll hear the door open and Reza come into the room. She says it would put her in the mood, music and candlelight. Then she takes off her jacket and throws it aside. Massimo presses a button. *Louder*, Blum says, drawing him away from the door into the middle of the room, leading him by the hand, making him turn. Not for a moment does he seem to suspect anything untoward. Massimo is just looking at her, wanting her, touching her. He puts out a hand to caress her cheek, and steps back for a moment; he wants to see her face. *You're so beautiful*, he says. Then he draws her close again. His head is very near hers; she is putting off the moment when she will have to kiss him, she will not kiss him until she sees Reza stealing into the room. She must delay Massimo until she is sure that Reza is there to get his tongue out of her mouth. Not much longer. They dance around the room, drinking each other in. See how he nuzzles her, see how he wants her. See Blum counting the seconds and thinking that they mustn't leave any traces behind, no blood, nothing to tell Massimo's colleagues that this is a crime scene. They will not suspect that a policeman has been knocked out and abducted; Massimo will simply collapse on the floor. Now.

Reza strikes him. At the very moment when her lips touch Massimo's for the last time. Reza is suddenly there; she sees his face, his anger, and the iron bar that takes away her fear. There is just the dull, heavy sound of Massimo falling as though Reza had flicked a switch. The clown loses consciousness and they set to work; they have no time to think, they mustn't linger here. Everything goes according to plan: they carry him to the garage and put him in the casket. Reza ties him up with the tape. There is no lid on the casket, so he can see where he is when he comes round. Blum goes back into the kitchen, empties the wine down the sink and washes the glasses. She meticulously wipes everything she has touched. She switches off the music and the light and leaves the house.

49

This time, they drive only five kilometers. No one stops them; there's nothing unusual about a hearse coming to a halt at a set of traffic lights; no one knows that a defenseless police officer is lying in a casket in the back, tightly bound with sticky tape. Everything is as it should be. Reza is driving, observing all the rules of the road. They steal through the city with their cargo: Massimo Dollinger, husband of Ute Dollinger, father to no one, police officer, criminal investigation department. Only they know that he is going to die, and within the next hour. Reza and Blum don't exchange a word. They ignore the fact that he has come round and is kicking the walls of the casket. That doesn't trouble them; nor does the fact that he is groaning now. However loudly he shouts, however afraid he is, she remembers that Dunya's fear was greater, and so was the fear felt by Ilena and Youn. It was much greater, wider, deeper, and it lasted so much longer than the time it takes to drive through the city. In the five minutes before Reza switches off the engine, Blum remembers everything she has seen, everything Dunya told Mark. The things Massimo did are beyond her comprehension.

They reach the parking lot just before midnight. There is no one there to take any notice; they park close to the gate, as they usually do. Corpses can be delivered outside opening hours; the undertakers have keys. Tonight the hearse will stay in the parking lot longer than usual, but no one will think anything of it, because no one comes here in the middle of the night. They feel calm here, on familiar terrain. For a long time Reza used to earn extra money doing shifts here, and he knows that the only CCTV cameras are trained on the main entrance. He also knows that they will be alone here all night. It is Friday, and the building has emptied for the weekend. No one will disturb them, no one will hear Massimo kicking up a fuss: good old Massimo. He hasn't figured out where they have brought him. He is bellowing furiously, but only groaning can be heard. He struggles in vain as they put him on a gurney and wheel him down a corridor into the main room. Slowly the truth is dawning. He desperately tries to sit up, his eyes cartoonishly wide when he sees the furnace, when he hears Blum say *This is the end of the line, you bastard.*

They are in Innsbruck crematorium. It is on the edge of the industrial park, a freestanding building where the dead turn to ash. It takes two and a half hours to cremate a body. Then the remains are taken out of the furnace; the nails, screws, pacemakers, and artificial joints are removed by magnet and thrown away; everything else goes in a grinder. Bits of bone that haven't burned right down, for instance, producing a sound like a coffee mill, but after a few minutes only fine ash is left. All in all, about two kilos of ash will remain, depending on the body's size and weight. The process is clean and effective, and it doesn't leave a trace of blood. Reza knows every process: he knows which button to press to open the furnace door and which to press to close it. He sits down at the computer for a moment and enters a number. The cremations are numbered consecutively, so he just reuses the number of the last one. No one will notice that Number 19,654 has been used twice. He smiles, because he knows that on Monday the head of the crematorium will open up, drink his coffee, read his newspaper, and remain completely oblivious. He will fetch the body from the cool room, enter 19,655 into the program, get the casket onto the hydraulic ramp, and press the button. He won't suspect a thing because nothing will remain of Massimo Dollinger.

They take the casket off the gurney and over to the hydraulic ramp. Blum observes his desperation, his rage and fear. He tries to break free, he flings his body back and forth, and the casket wobbles as it rises in the air. It stops at chest height. Massimo turns his scarlet face to Blum, a defenseless, panic-stricken monster with eyes ablaze. All he can move is his head, ninety degrees to the left, ninety degrees to the right. However much he wants to leap up and attack her, he can't. All he can do is talk: tell the truth, humiliate himself, beg for forgiveness. Blum comes very close and whispers that he is about to die. *In five minutes' time you'll be burning. You can keep shouting or you can talk to me. The decision is yours.* She withdraws her face from his and stands there, watching him compose himself. How quickly he transforms. He calms his body and waits for her to tear off the sticky tape. Massimo knows he must do as she says, he knows he mustn't make a false move, mustn't provoke her. His eyes wander back and forth, he is feverishly thinking. Blum knows him well. He'd do anything to save his skin, he will talk for his life.

"Why, Massimo?"

"I'm so sorry, Blum."

"That's not what I want to hear."

"If I could turn the clock back—"

"Stop it."

"You must believe me. Mark was my friend."

"For the last time, this is not what I want to hear."

"What do you want to hear, then?"

"Why the cellar?"

"It just happened, Blum."

"Happened?"

"It happened by chance. The neighbors called the police. I was in Kitzbühel on a surveillance mission. I thought I'd give my uniformed colleagues a hand, and I followed up the call."

"When was this?"

"Four and a half years ago."

"Were you on your own?"

"It was the middle of the night, I was awake anyway, so I thought I'd go and see what was up for myself."

"And what was up?"

"The neighbors had heard screams."

"Yes?"

"I rang the bell, I knocked on the door, then I climbed in. The cellar window was open."

"Go on."

"They were raping her, four of them. Men with their trousers down wearing masks. They'd left the window open by mistake, and the girl was screaming so loudly that she could be heard from the street. She wouldn't stop screaming. I didn't know what to do. I had to keep the men in my sights; I shouldn't have answered the call alone. I was in extreme circumstances, Blum."

"So what *did* you do?"

"I hit her on the head with my gun."

"Why?"

"I had no option."

"So instead of helping her, you hit her?"

"I wanted to shut her up. I had to get the situation under control, and I was afraid the four men might attack me. They were wearing masks. I was afraid, Blum."

"You had a gun."

"I panicked."

"Which of them was it? Dunya or Ilena?"

"Ilena."

"And you didn't help her."

"No, I didn't."

"Why not?"

"I don't know."

Blum listens to what he has to say. He is trying to justify his decision to stay, not to call for reinforcements but to talk to the men. He talked to them upstairs in the deserted restaurant while Ilena was lying unconscious and anesthetized below. When they removed their masks, Massimo simply closed the doors and windows and went back to the outside world. He turned a blind eye, then he let temptation lead him. He'd seen the land of Cockaigne, a secret place where everything was permitted and he answered to no one. In this place, he couldn't hear Ute wailing that God had overlooked them, that her life was pointless without a child. He talks about Ute, about how she rejected him and wouldn't let him touch her, how she made him feel it was all his fault. Her husband wasn't a real man, he was a failure who couldn't even give her a child. She told him so every day, and the humiliation made his life unbearable. *It only happened because of the trouble with Ute*, he said. That was what caused his false move that night in the cellar.

Massimo is lying in his spruce casket on the verge of tears. His mouth opens and closes, and Blum watches Mark's eternally kind, helpful friend. His voice is calm, he sounds almost meek, you would never imagine that he is capable of what he did. That he bought himself a brightly colored mask and returned to the captives' tormentors. He had them in the palm of his hand: it was easy to come to an agreement with the priest and the cook, the huntsman and the photographer. They did as he asked; they accepted this new member of their club. Four became five and all because they had forgotten to close a window.

His eyes lock with hers, as though somehow he can latch on to her and haul himself up. They are small, sad eyes, as unimpressive as everything else about him. Briefly, the monster is calm, briefly the kindliness is back, for a moment she even pities him for being who he is. But only for a moment. She tries to remind herself of the old times, when the world was still intact. There is a wild beast slumbering behind those eyes, prowling up and down, scraping its hooves in the sand, ready to bite. It would pounce and rip into her throat without hesitation.

But he knows the beast cannot attack; he sees in her face that it makes no difference what he says. It's over. He hears the resolution in every word she speaks. Blum wants him to die. In her cold, hard stare, he sees there is no way out. So the wind changes again and the storm inside him rises. The wild beast of his fury returns.

"What happened to the others?"
"They're dead."
"I don't believe you're capable of that, Blum."
"That was precisely your mistake."
"You killed them?"
"I got them ready for their funerals."
"No."
"Yes."
"You think you're any better than me?"
"I do."
"Well, you're wrong."

"You hit and kicked the girl until she lost her baby. She bled to death. And then you just threw her away."

"And you decapitated a priest."

"Yes, and now I'm going to burn you."

"You won't go through with this."

"I will, for Mark."

"Blum, this is ridiculous."

"You were the worst of them all."

"That's what your little friend told you, did she?"

"Yes."

"If she'd only kept her mouth shut she'd still be alive. I wouldn't have had to hold her head underwater. She wouldn't have ended up in the River Inn like the boy."

"You bastard."

"It's a shame we had to close our little club. Your husband and that little cunt insisted on trying to save the day."

"Stop."

"I had a lot of fun with Dunya, the little slut. We were very fond of her. It was silly of her to run away."

"I told you to stop."

"I was very surprised to see her in the girls' bedroom after I'd fucked you. There was no keeping that little whore down."

"I said—"

"She was really good in the sack, believe me. I'm sure Mark would have told you the same."

"Stop!"

"Oh no, that's not all—"

She doesn't want to hear another word, she doesn't want to know a thing more, she wants to be rid of him. Her finger depresses the button and he begins to scream. The furnace door opens and the casket slides in, feetfirst. Massimo roars but no one can hear his curses, no one can come to his aid. Blum and Reza stand side by side, fingers intertwined, watching the spectacle unfold. They don't move; they do nothing to stop what is coming next, they just stand hand in hand watching the furnace door. How Massimo screams, but only for a moment. Then everything is still, and suddenly it's just the two of them.

It is the middle of the night and they are getting used to the feeling that everything will be all right. He burns for two hours. They sit on the floor in front of the furnace, waiting. They don't talk but they are still holding hands. From time to time Blum gets up and looks through the window to get a glimpse of Massimo's disintegrating body. As she watches the fire rage at 750 degrees, she gets the sense that life will become easier. They reemerge into the night and drive along the highway. Nothing is left of Massimo but ashes in a plastic bag. By the time they stop at the service station, she is convinced that she will survive. She drops him into the dirty toilet and flushes him away.

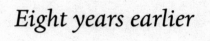

Eight years earlier

"Blum?"

"Yes."

"May I ask you something?"

"Anything you like."

"Afterwards, we don't ever have to talk about it again."

"About what?"

"You know I'm on your side. Always have been, always will be. But you've got to tell me the truth."

"You're scaring me, Mark."

"Everything's all right, Blum."

"Is it? You sound odd. What is it?"

"I want to know if you had a reason."

"I don't understand."

"Whether they deserved it."

"What are you talking about?"

"Your parents."

"What about them?"

"Did they deserve to drown?"

"What do you mean?"

"I just want you to tell me that it had to happen. That they deserved to die. Tell me. That's all I want to know."

"Please stop this, Mark."

"I love you, Blum. You know that. But you must answer me."

"Why?"

"Because I don't want to feel afraid."

"Of me?"

"Yes, of you. And if you tell me there was a reason then I can understand. Understand you. And what you did. Please tell me, Blum."

"How long have you known?"

"I've known all along. I could read it in your eyes."

"You're a police officer."

"I'm going to be your husband. And that's why I have to know. I promise, I'll never mention it again. But just this once tell me why."

"They drowned."

"I want to live with you, Blum, and someday I want us to have children."

"And first you want to be sure I'm not a monster."

"Correct."

"I had a hundred reasons, Mark. It had to happen."

"Did it?"

"They deserved it. It's better that they're dead. Believe me."

"That's okay, then."

"Is it?"

"Yes, Blum."

"You're not going to leave me?"

"I'm not going leave you."

"Are you sure?"

"Positive."

About the Author

Bernhard Aichner is an award-winning author and photographer living in Innsbruck, Austria. His books have been translated into twelve languages. *Woman of the Dead* is his first book to be translated into English.

NORTHVILLE DISTRICT LIBRARY

3 9082 12814 9484